Red Spy at Night

Blade stepped over the cot and reached the officer while the Russian was still on his knees. He flicked his right foot up and out, connecting, slamming his instep into the Russian's ribs, knocking the officer onto his back.

"Blade! Stop!" Plato cried.

Blade's left hand grabbed the gasping officer under the chin. He squeezed and lifted, his arm bulging, hauling the Russian from the cement floor and into the air.

Plato went to grip Blade's arm, but Geronimo quickly stepped between them, shaking his head.

Blade drew his right Bowie and pressed the tip into the Russian's genitals.

The officer squirmed and thrashed, wheezing, his eyes bulging.

Blade paused, his gray eyes boring into the officer's. "You killed two of my Family, you son of a bitch!"

Also in the *Endworld* series:

THE FOX RUN
THIEF RIVER FALLS RUN
TWIN CITIES RUN
KALISPELL RUN
DAKOTA RUN
CITADEL RUN
ARMAGEDDON RUN
DENVER RUN
CAPITAL RUN
NEW YORK RUN

DAVID ROBBINS

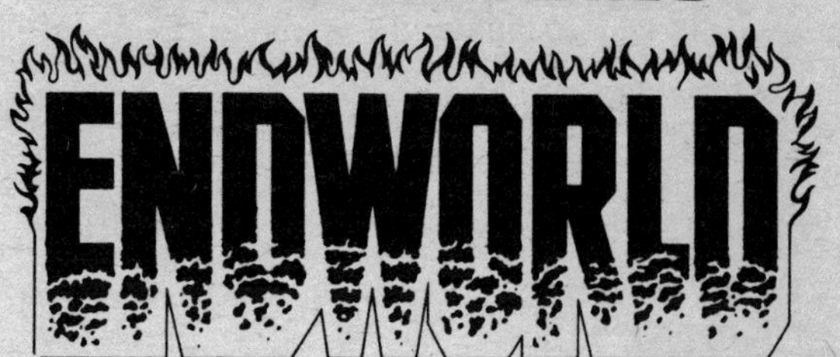

LIBERTY RUN

LEISURE BOOKS NEW YORK CITY

Dedicated to . . .
Judy and Joshua and the one in the oven,
& Socrates,
George Gordon Lord Byron,
and Mighty Mouse.

A LEISURE BOOK

Published by

Dorchester Publishing Co., Inc.
6 East 39th Street
New York, New York 10016

Printed in the United States of America

ENDWORLD

Warrior Roll

ALPHA TRIAD
Blade
Hickok
Geronimo

BETA TRIAD
Rikki-Tikki-Tavi
Yama
Teucer

GAMMA TRIAD
Spartacus
Shane
Bertha

OMEGA TRIAD
Ares
Helen
Sundance

ZULU TRIAD
Samson
Sherry
Marcus

1

Three women emerged from the compound.

"Look!" exclaimed the stockiest of the five soldiers hidden in the forest to the west.

"I see," said the leader of the quintet, a lean lieutenant with angular facial features. His brown eyes narrowed.

"Do we take them, Lieutenant Lysenko?" asked the third of the five men. Each of them wore a brown uniform; each of them was a seasoned professional; each carried an AK-47.

Lieutenant Lysenko nodded.

"It is big, is it not?" commented another soldier, a handsome, youthful trooper wearing his helmet cocked at an angle.

Lieutenant Lysenko, keeping his attention fixed on the trio of women 150 yards away, nodded. "The Home embraces a thirty-acre plot," he noted absently.

"The Home!" The stocky soldier snickered. "What a stupid name!"

"I don't know about that," Lieutenant Lysenko remarked. "I sort of like it. The man responsible for constructing that walled compound knew what he was doing. His name was Kurt Carpenter, according to the files our informant turned over to us. Carpenter was no fool. He foresaw the inevitability of World War Three and took appropriate action. For an American, he was most unusual. Not at all like the typical capitalistic swine of his time. He used his wealth to build this place he called the Home, then gathered a select group here shortly before the war. He dubbed them his Family."

"The Home! The Family!" the stocky soldier said, his tone laced with scorn. "I still think it's stupid!"

Lieutenant Lysenko cast a disapproving glance at the trooper. "Were your feeble intellect the equal of your flippant mouth, Grozny, the Party Congress would hail you as a genius," he stated acidly.

Private Grozny frowned, but held his tongue. He knew better than to match wits with the cerebral Lysenko. He also knew what would happen if he riled the officer.

The approaching women were 125 yards off.

"Was it stupid of Kurt Carpenter to surround his compound with twenty-foot-high brick walls?" Lieutenant Lysenko demanded. "And to cap those thick walls with barbed wire? Or to install a sturdy, massive drawbridge in the center of the west wall as the only means of entering or exiting to minimize hostile penetration? Was it stupid of him to initiate the practice of designating certain Family members as Warriors, superbly trained individuals responsible for preserving the Home and safeguarding the Family?"

"No," Grozny admitted.

"It was very smart of them to clear the fields all around their Home," interjected the youngest soldier.

"True," Lysenko said. "Our task is that much more difficult."

Grozny nodded at the women. "The mice come to the cats, eh?"

Lieutenant Lysenko studied one of the women. "But one of the mice sports fangs," he observed.

One of the women was armed. She was a tall blonde with prominent cheekbones, thin lips, and an intent expression. A brown shirt and green pants, both patched in several spots, covered her athletic form. Moccasins adorned her small feet.

"What kind of guns are those?" asked the youthful trooper.

"I don't know," Lysenko acknowledged.

"They arm their women?" Grozny inquired.

"What is so surprising about that?" Lieutenant Lysenko countered. "We have female soldiers in our army."

"Do you think the blonde is a Warrior?" queried the young soldier.

Lieutenant Lysenko scratched his chin, reflecting. He

had not considered the possibility of the woman being a Warrior, and he mentally chided himself for his neglect. An officer could not afford to overlook any eventuality. The mission's success and the lives of his squad depended on his perception and judgment.

"Orders?" Grozny questioned him.

The five soldiers were concealed behind trees and brush a few yards from the edge of the forest, from the end of the field.

"Move back," Lysenko instructed them. "You know the drill. And remember. General Malenkov wants a live prisoner. We will take the blonde."

"And the other two?" Grozny mentioned.

"Kill them," Lysenko directed.

The quintet melted into the foliage, Grozny and the young trooper drawing their bayonets as they blended into the bushes.

The unsuspecting women neared the tree line, the blonde in the lead. Her alert green eyes scanned the forest, probing for mutates, mutants, raiding scavengers, or any other menace. She detected a slight movement deep in the trees and stopped.

"Is something wrong?" asked one of the women behind her, a brunette wearing a faded yellow blouse and tan pants.

"I'll tell you what's wrong," quipped the third woman. She was exceptionally slim and wore a blue shirt and pants, both garments having been constructed for her by the Family Weavers. "Sherry's a Warrior."

"What's that have to do with anything?" inquired the brunette.

The third woman ran her right hand through her black hair. "Warriors are walking bundles of nerves," she said. "They have to be, in their line of work. She probably heard a twig snap, and can't decide if it's a bunny rabbit or a monster!"

"Quiet," Sherry declared.

"Give me a . . ." the black-haired woman started to speak, but the brunette gripped her right arm and motioned for silence.

Sherry raised her M.A.C. 10, listening. All she could

hear was the breeze rustling the leaves of the trees, an unusually warm breeze for an October day. The leaves were red and yellow and orange, resplendent in their fall colors. She couldn't see anything out of the ordinary, but her intuition was nagging at her mind, and over the years she'd learned to rely on her feminine intuition. It was seldom wrong.

"Should we return to the Home?" whispered the brunette.

Sherry bit her lower lip and glanced over her right shoulder at the Home. Blade's orders had been specific: escort a pair of novice Healers into the forest and guard them while they searched for wild herbs. The assignment was far from critical. But how would Blade react when he learned she'd aborted the search because of a vague troubling premonition? She decided to proceed, but cautiously. "We'll keep going," she informed the pair behind her. "But stick close to me. Don't wander off."

The brunette nodded.

The third woman rolled her brown eyes skyward.

Sherry advanced toward the woods. She could feel the comforting pressure of her Smith and Wesson .357 Combat Magnum in its holster on her right hip.

Somewhere in the depths of the northwestern Minnesota forest a bird chirped.

Sherry paused when she reached the end of the field, peering between the trunks of the trees and into the shadows of the pines.

"Let's get this over with," said the black-haired woman. Like the brunette, she was 20 years of age. Unlike the brunette, she had applied to become a Healer at her mother's insistence and not due to any innate sense of altruism.

Sherry stared at the impatient neophyte. "When I tell you to be quiet," she informed her, "you'll shut your mouth or I'll shut it for you. Understand?"

The black-haired woman bristled. "Who do you think you are, talking to me like that?"

"As you pointed out," Sherry said, "I'm a Warrior, Claudia. And as such, in times of danger, what I say goes."

"Danger?" Claudia scoffed. "What danger? Are we going to be molested by a moth?"

"Claudia!" the brunette spoke up. "Sherry is right, and you know it."

"Nobody tells me what to do, Jean!" Claudia snapped. Before Sherry or Jean could intervene, she angrily stomped into the forest.

Jean stepped up to Sherry. "Don't take her outburst personally. Claudia is upset because she knows she won't be accepted as a Healer. Our apprenticeship, our probationary period, is over in a week. And there's no way Claudia will be certified."

Sherry watched Claudia disappear behind a broad pine tree. "Why did the Elders even accept her as a trainee? She's too damn immature to be a Healer."

Jean shrugged. "You know the Elders. They probably wanted her to at least have a chance at it."

"And her mother is real close to Kant, and Kant was the Elder who recommended Claudia for Healer status," Sherry stated.

Jean seemed shocked by the implication. "The Elders would never allow anyone to unduly influence their judgment."

Sherry started walking into the woods. "The Elders aren't infallible," she said over her left shoulder.

Jean stayed on Sherry's heels. "If you'd been born in the Family, you'd never make such an accusation."

Sherry's lips tightened. True, she'd been born and raised in Canada, in a small town called Sundown located across the border from Minnesota. True too was the fact her nomination and acceptance as a Warrior could be attributed to the influence exerted by her husband, the Family's preeminent gunfighter, the Warrior known as Hickok. Perhaps, if she had been reared in the close-knit Family, she wouldn't presume to question an Elder's integrity. Jean's mild rebuke stung her, and for a few moments she was distracted, weighing the validity of the reproof instead of concentrating on the vegetation around them, on their immediate situation.

The mistake cost her.

"Where did Claudia go?" Jean asked.

The query brought Sherry out of herself. She searched the landscape ahead. "Claudia! Where are you?" she called out.

Claudia didn't answer.

"Knowing Claudia's temper the way I do," Jean mentioned, "she might just ignore you."

"She does," Sherry said, "and she'll live to regret it."

"Claudia!" Jean shouted. "Come back here!"

Sherry moved past a large pine, then up a low incline. She reached the top of the mound and glanced down. And froze.

Claudia was lying on her back at the base of the grassy mound. Her throat was slit, and blood was gushing from her neck and flowing down the front of her blue shirt and spilling over her shoulders. Her wide, lifeless eyes gaped at the azure sky.

Jean bumped into Sherry, then spotted the corpse. "Dear Spirit!" she exclaimed, horrified. "Claudia!"

Sherry twisted and shoved Jean from the mound. "Run!" she ordered. "Head for the Home!"

Jean hesitated, too stunned by Claudia's death to realize her own danger.

But Sherry knew. Her intuition had been right! Some menace was lurking in the woods! And whoever had slain Claudia had to be nearby, ready to pounce again! She crouched, cradling the M.A.C. 10.

Not a moment too soon.

A soldier in a brown uniform burst from the brush seven yards to her right.

In the instant Sherry spied him, she recognized the uniform as belonging to a Russian trooper, and knew the gun in his hand was an AK-47. Hickok had told her all about his experiences in the Capital, when he'd been captured by the Russians. Her mind processed the information in the split second it took her to react, and her finger squeezed the trigger when the Russian was still six yards off.

The Soviet soldier was stopped in midstride as the

slugs tore through his chest. His ears never heard the metallic chattering of the M.A.C. 10, because he was dead before the sound could reach them. He toppled to the hard ground without uttering a word.

Sherry swiveled, knowing there would be more, and there was another one, coming at her from her left, holding the barrel of his AK-47 as if it were a club, his legs pounding up the mound, and she fired when he was only two feet from her. The M.A.C. 10 caught him in the face, and he was flipped backwards by the impact, sprawling onto his back and sliding to a halt against a tree.

Jean!

Sherry spun, hoping the Russians hadn't gone after the aspiring Healer, but she was too late.

A stocky soldier had grabbed Jean from the rear. His left arm was clamped around her neck, while his right plunged a bayonet into her body again and again and again.

Sherry was about to let him have it in the head, when she heard the padding of rushing feet behind her. She whirled, but before she could complete the turn someone plowed into her and bore her to the earth. Strong arms gripped her wrists, preventing her from using the M.A.C. 10. She glimpsed a youthful face above her, and then something was pressed over her nose and mouth, something soft with a slight odor. Sherry heaved and strained, attempting to buck her captor, but another set of hands grabbed her shoulders and held her fast.

"We have her!" someone exulted.

Sherry's senses were swimming. She tried to focus, to use the martial fighting skills taught to her by Rikki-Tikki-Tavi, but her sluggish mind refused to obey her mental commands. Gasping, she made one last valiant effort to rise, then lost consciousness.

"We have her!" Grozny repeated, still holding her shoulders.

The young trooper, straddling her waist, nodded.

Lieutenant Lysenko, crouched to her right, removed the chloroform-soaked white cloth from her face and stood. "We must leave right away!"

"What's the hurry?" Grozny asked. "Shouldn't we bury our comrades first?"

"Fool!" Lysenko barked. "Do you want to end up like them?" He pointed to the two dead men. "The Family will have heard the shooting in the Home! They will send their Warriors after us!" He paused and gazed at the unconsious blonde. "She is quite formidable. If the other Warriors are half as good as her, we are in trouble! Come! Grozny, you carry her. Serov, you take the lead. We must reach the rendezvous point and signal for the copter to come and pick us up."

Serov grabbed his AK-47 from the ground where it had fallen, then hurried to the southeast.

Grozny grunted as he draped the blonde's body over his left shoulder. He retrieved his AK-47, clutching it in his right hand.

"Go!" Lysenko directed. "I will cover you." He picked up his AK-47 and waited while Grozny hastened into the trees. So far, so good. They had the live captive General Malenkov wanted. Leaving the dead men behind was regrettable, but it could not be helped. The Family would learn who was responsible for taking one of their vaunted Warriors, but what could they do about it? Nothing. According to the files relayed by the spy in Denver, the family only numbered about seven dozen members. Only 15 of them were Warriors. And 15 fighters, no matter how adept at their craft they might be, could hardly hope to oppose the military might of the Union of Soviet Socialist Republics.

Loud voices arose from the direction of the Home.

Lysenko followed his men, constantly surveying the foliage behind him, alert for any hint of pursuit. He thought of the reception awaiting him in Washington, and he was pleased. This mission would definitely boost his career, perhaps lead to a speedy promotion. Maybe an assignment on General Malenkov's personal staff. The prospect was exciting. General Malenkov was a man of considerable stature in the North American Central Committee, responsible for administering the occupational forces in America. The Soviets had been fortunate during the war; they'd been able to invade and hold a sizeable segment of the eastern U.S. New England, a portion of New York, southern Pennsylvania, Maryland, New Jersey, southern Ohio, southern Indiana, parts of Illinois, Kentucky, Virginia, and West Virginia, as well as sections of North and South Carolina were all under Soviet hegemony. The Soviets had intended to conquer the entire country, but their drive through Alaska and Canada had been stopped. And their push into the deep South had been resisted every step of the way, and eventually halted, by the determined Southerners.

Now, over a century since World War III, the status of the Soviet occupation was still the same. Slightly over 30 years ago, the Russians in America had lost contact with their Motherland. Ships sent to investigate the reason had never returned. Planes had vanished. Communications had gone unanswered. To maintain their military rule, the American-based Soviets had instituted a program of forcibly impregnating selected American women, then training and educating their children, indoctrinating them, creating devoted Communists every bit as loyal as any ever born on Russian soil.

In other areas, the Russians had encountered severe problems. Much of American's industrial might had been crippled during the war, and the Soviets suffered shortages in everything from food to military hardware. Their expansion plans to the west had been thwarted by the Civilized Zone Army. During the war, after a neutron bomb was dropped on Washington, what was left of the United States Government had withdrawn to Denver, Colorado, and reorganized under the direction of a man named Samuel Hyde, the Secretary of Health, Education, and Welfare. Hyde had implemented Executive Order 11490, a law few Americans had ever known existed, enabling him to assume dictatorial control of the area under his domination, the area subsequently dubbed the Civilized Zone. Hyde's bloodline had ruled the Civilized Zone for a century.

Then the incredible had happened. The tiny Family

had defeated the last of the dictators and his cohort, the infamous scientist known as the Doktor, and precious freedom had been restored to the people of the Civilized Zone. According to the files Lysenko had read, the Family had been aided in their epic struggle by several factions. One was an army of superb horsemen from South Dakota called the Cavalry. Another contingent of fighters had come from the subterranean city designated the Mound, located many miles east of the Home. Refugees from the ravaged Twin Cities of Minneapolis and St. Paul, calling themselves the Clan, had abetted the Warriors, as had the Flathead Indians from Montana. Afterwards, these six groups had formed into the Freedom Federation, pledging to present a united front to any adversaries and to work toward wresting the country from the savage barbarism prevalent since the collapse of civilization.

Which worried the Soviets no end. General Malenkov and the other Russian leaders viewed the Freedom Federation as their primary enemy, to be eliminated at all costs, no matter what steps might be necessary. The Family was considered to be the soul of the Freedom Federation; they were the smallest numerically, yet they exerted the greatest influence in the Freedom Federation councils. The files the spy had sent contained extensive information on the Family, but not enough to satisfy General Malenkov. He'd ordered a squad sent to capture a Family member, and then truth serum could extract pertinent information detailing the Family's exploitable weaknesses.

And here I am, Lieutenant Lysenko mentally noted as he hurried after Grozny and Serov.

Several sparrows suddenly flew from a dense bush 20 yards to the rear.

Lysenko stopped, training his AK-47 on the bush, waiting.

Nothing else happened.

Lieutenant Lysenko jogged to the southeast. He knew General Malenkov viewed this assignment as being critically important, especially in light of the recent fiasco in Philadelphia. The Soviets could not afford to conduct campaigns on two fronts. The Family's destruction was imperative. The Family was the unifying element in the Freedom Federation. Without the wise guidance of the Family, the Freedom Federation would fall apart. Or so General Malenkov believed. But how to accomplish the Family's elimination? Lysenko had participated in two policy sessions. Some high-ranking officers had wanted to send in a large force and wipe out the Family in one fell swoop. But this had been tried before, and it had signally failed. Others had advocated bombing the Home or using long-range missiles, but this idea contained crucial flaws. Soviet planes and jets were in disrepair, incapable of flying the tremendous distance involved. Their helicopters were marginally functional, too unreliable to undertake a full-scale assault of the compound. None of the aerial means, including missiles, could deliver a payload guaranteed to demolish a 30-acre expanse. And General Malenkov did not want any survivors, any martyrs to stir up the Freedom Federation. So Malenkov had proposed using deadly chemical weapons. To be completely effective, the Russians needed to know the layout of the Home, something their spy had been unable to uncover.

All of this passed through Lieutenant Lysenko's mind as he sprinted up a low hill. Fate had smiled on him. If he could pull this off, General Malenkov would be duly impressed. And when an officer was in Malenkov's favor, the sky was the limit as far as his career was concerned. Lysenko grinned. He would give anything to please his superior.

Lysenko reached the top of the hill and stopped, glancing back. He thought of the sparrows, and he wondered if they were being pursued. Except for the startled birds, there had been no other indication of anyone on their trail. The Warriors might be exceptionally competent, but it was doubtful they could chase someone through the thick forest without making *some* noise. The muted snap of a twig, or the faint rustle of a branch, could betray the stealthiest of professionals. Perfect silence, at the speed Serov, Grozny, and him were maintaining, was virtually impossible.

Or was it?

Lieutenant Lysenko started down the far side of the hill, bothered by a fact from the files he had neglected in the excitement of the moment.

What about the genetic deviates?

The brilliant Doktor had specialized in genetic engineering, in creating unique test-tube offspring, creatures combining human and animal qualities, aberrations endowed with bestial senses, yet governed by a rational intellect. Three of these genetic deviates, according to the files, now resided with the Family, had actually joined the Family in its fight with the Doktor, rebelling against their demented creator. Lysenko had heard other tales about the deviates, about their grotesque appearance and extraordinary abilities, even reports the deviates consumed humans. He quickened his pace.

The minutes dragged by.

The helicopter had deposited the squad ten miles to the southeast of the Home, in a spacious clearing in the woods. Lysenko had hidden their radio before departing for the Home. The helicopter had returned to Decatur for refueling and to await their transmission signifying their mission was completed.

Lieutenant Lysenko spotted Grozny and Serov 40 yards ahead, waiting. He ran to join them.

Grozny was on one knee, breathing heavily, the blonde on the ground beside him.

Serov was leaning against a tree, scanning the nearby vegetation.

"Why have you stopped?" Lieutenant Lysenko demanded as he reached them.

Grozny looked up. "I have carried her eight miles, sir. I am fatigued."

Lysenko frowned. "You can rest when we get to the rendezvous point. Not before. On your feet!"

Grozny slowly stood, his left hand held to his side. "So sorry, comrade, but I have a pain."

"You are becoming soft, Grozny," Lysenko snapped.

Grozny resented the insult. "Soft? Who else could carry over a hundred pounds for eight miles?"

"I could," chimed in a new voice.

The Russians whirled.

There were three of them, calmly standing between two trees, not more than ten yards to the west. The one on the right was the tallest, about five feet ten, and humanoid in aspect. The creature was naked except for a brown loincloth. Its skin was gray and leathery. A hawklike skull dominated its squat neck. Its nose was pointed, its ears no more than tiny circles of flesh on either side of its bald head. The mouth was a thin slit. The eyes contained bizarre, bright red pupils. Its expression reflected its nervousness.

The one on the left wore a black loincloth, and its feral features radiated sheer animosity. This deviate only reached four feet in height, and couldn't have weighed more than 60 pounds. Brown hair, about three inches in length, covered its entire body. Its head was outsized for its diminutive form. A long, tapered nose almost resembled a snout. Beady brown eyes shifted from trooper to trooper.

In the center was the smallest deviate, just shy of four feet tall, but weighing about as much as the feral one. A thick coat of short, grayish-brown hair or fur encased his wiry physique. A gray loincloth protected his genitals. His eyes were vivid green and slightly slanted. His ears were pointed. He resembled, for all the world, a living cat-man. Pointed nails capped his bony fingers. Amazingly, his posture conveyed a supreme nonchalance. He was even grinning, exposing his needlelike teeth. "Hi, there, chuckles!" he said to Lysenko in a high-pitched, lisping voice. "We're the Three Musketeers. I'm Athos. This"—he indicated his tall companion—"is Aramis. And this"—he nodded at the feral one—"is Porthos. We're here to shish-kebab your gonads!"

Lieutenant Lysenko recovered quickly. His initial stupefaction subsided, and he leveled his AK-47 and squeezed the trigger.

Too late.

The three . . . things . . . darted from view, taking cover behind the trees, moving with astonishing speed. One moment they were there; the next they were gone.

Lysenko's burst struck the two trees, splintering the wood, sending chips flying. He ceased firing, glancing at Grozny, jerked his head to the left.

Grozny nodded and crouched, stepping to the left of the trees.

Lysenko motioned for Serov to do likewise to the right. He waited while his men cautiously neared the trees from opposite sides, prepared to catch the genetic deviates in a cross fire.

Grozny and Serov paused, exchanged glances, and swept around the trees, weapons at the ready.

"Well?" Lysenko barked when they failed to fire.

"They're gone!" Grozny exclaimed.

"Gone? Where could they go?" Lysenko queried in disbelief.

Harsh laughter sounded from the wall of forest beyond.

Grozny and Serov backpedaled to Lysenko's side.

"What are they?" Serov hissed.

"Mutants," Lieutenant Lysenko answered. "Man-made mutants."

"They're dead mutants if they show their faces again," Grozny vowed.

From in the woods came a low, raspy question: "Should I be scared now, or later?"

More laughter.

"What do we do?" Serov asked in a soft whisper.

"You can drop your guns and give up!" ordered the one with the high, lisping voice, the cat-man. "And we'll let you live!"

"You are insane!" Lysenko shouted. "You don't even carry guns!"

The cat-man snickered. "I don't need a gun, bub! My nails will slice you open like a rotten melon!"

Grozny was peering into the vegetation. "Where the hell are they? I can't see them!"

Lieutenant Lysenko looked at the blonde. Inspiration struck. "I know you come from the Home!" he shouted. "I know what you are!"

"I think we've just been insulted," said the low, raspy voice, seemingly coming from a tangle of brush to the left.

"If you don't come out now," Lieutenant Lysenko warned, "I will kill our prisoner!"

"I wouldn't do that, dimples, if I were you!" yelled the cat-man. "Her hubby is after your ass, and he's one mad son of a gun. His name is Hickok. Maybe you've heard of him? He's got quite a rep. I expect he'll jam his Colt Pythons up your butt and keep pullin' the triggers until the cylinders are empty!"

"I'm serious!" Lysenko repeated his threat. "I'll kill her!"

The cat-man uttered a peculiar trilling sound. "Not nice, chuckles! Not nice at all!"

Silence descended.

"Do you think they've gone?" Serov asked hopefully.

"Come out!" Lysenko bellowed.

"Please!" cried a new voice, coming from directly ahead. "Surrender, yes? Avoid bloodshed, no?"

Lieutenant Lysenko was stymied. He could hear the deviates, but couldn't see them. And he couldn't shoot what he couldn't see. He was bluffing about killing the blonde, because General Malenkov needed her alive. Lysenko suspected the damn mutants were deliberately delaying their escape, hindering them until the Warriors could arrive.

"What do we do, sir?" Serov asked anxiously.

Before Lysenko could reply, a high-pitched voice, from directly behind them, answered, "I say we play peekaboo!"

The Russians soldiers spun.

The cat-man and the feral one were already in motion. The cat-man leaped onto Grozny, burying the tapered tips of his right fingernails in Grozny's eyes, even as his left hand, his fingers pressed together, forming a compact point, speared into Grozny's throat. Grozny screamed as the cat-man tore his eyeballs from their sockets and ripped his neck from chin to chest.

Serov bravely endeavored to bring his AK-47 into play as the feral creature landed on his chest in one bound. Snarling, the deviate placed a hairy hand on either side of Serov's astounded face, then brutally wrenched Serov's head to the left. There was a distinct popping noise, and Serov slumped to the ground.

Lieutenant Lysenko had retreated several steps, unable to fire without hitting Grozny and Serov. He aimed at the feral one as Serov fell, but before he could shoot, the third mutant intervened. Steely gray arms encircled him, lifted him from the ground. The pressure was unbelievable. He felt like his chest was on the verge of being crushed. His AK-47 clattered to the earth.

The feral one was standing with its arms folded, smirking, staring at Serov.

The cat-man suddenly rose from Grozny's body, its hands soaked with blood, dripping crimson. It grinned, then glared at Lysenko. "Put the Red down, Gremlin," he said. "I want to have some fun."

Gremlin twisted his torso, holding the soldier away from his feline friend. "No, Lynx! Blade wanted them alive, yes? Must spare this one, no?"

Lynx shook his head, his ears twitching. "I just want to have a little fun with him."

"Bet me!" interjected the feral one in his low, rasping tone. "I've seen that look in your eyes before. You've got the blood lust."

"Who asked you, Ferret?" Lynx quipped.

"I know what I'm talking about," Ferret persisted. "All of us are prone to it. Maybe its part of our genetic constitution. You know as well as I that the damn Doktor designed us as his personal assassin corps."

"Yeah," Lynx concurred. "The Doc was always braggin' about being the only person able to edit the genetic instructions encoded in DNA, or some such garbage. Odds are, he intended for us to live to kill."

Gremlin shook his leathery head. "Gremlin has never had blood lust, yes? Must not be true for all of us, no?"

Lynx snickered. "Gremlin, you're such a goody-goody, you'd never kill anyone or anything just for the thrill of it."

Gremlin frowned. "There is a thrill in killing, yes?"

"For some of us," Lynx confessed. He nodded at the Red. "You're real lucky, pal. If I hadn't of given my word to Blade, you'd be mincemeat right about now."

"Listen!" Ferret exclaimed.

There was a crashing in the underbrush, and a man dashed into view, breathing heavily from the strenuous exertion of having run eight miles. He was a lean blond, with a sweeping handlebar mustache. Buckskins and moccasins covered his muscular frame. Strapped around his waist were a pair of pearl-handled Colt Python revolvers.

"Hickok!" Lynx declared. "We're having a pajama party! Care to join us?"

The gunman ignored the comment. His blue eyes swept the area, and locked on the unconscious figure of his wife. He ran up to her.

Lynx glanced at Ferret. "Is this what they mean by true love?"

Hickok knelt by Sherry's side and cradled her in his arms. He carefully examined her but couldn't find any visible injury.

"Sherry is fine, yes?" Gremlin asked hopefully.

"She'd best be," Hickok growled. He took her in his arms, then stood.

"Do you need some help?" Ferret asked.

Hickok shook his head. He walked over to the Russian officer, his seething eyes pinpoints of fury. "If you've hurt her, you bastard, you're dead! Nothing will keep me from you! No one will stop me! I'll kill you inch by miserable inch, until you beg for mercy! You understand me?"

Lieutenant Lysenko scowled.

Lynx looked at Ferret, beaming. "I love it when he talks like that!"

Hickok leaned toward the Russian. "You wipe that off your face, or I'll kill you right now!"

"Hickok!"

The speaker was new to the scene, a giant of a man, striding toward them, his massive arms and legs bulging with raw power. His hair was dark, his eyes a piercing gray, his complexion rugged. He wore a black leather vest and green fatigue pants, as well as moccasins, the typical Family footwear. A pair of Bowies, his favorite weapons, rested in their sheaths, one on each hip.

"Uh-oh!" Lynx declared. "The party-pooper is here!"

"I need him alive," the big man said to Hickok.

Hickok's lips compressed. He glanced at the giant, then nodded. "Fine by me, Blade, but I want him when you're through."

"That's not up to me," Blade said, "and you know it."

Hickok gazed at the soldier. "I'll be seein' you." He walked off, Sherry nestled in his arms.

Blade studied the dead men, then stared at Lynx. "I thought I told you I wanted them alive."

Lynx shrugged. "Couldn't be helped. Besides, we did save you one of them."

Blade moved over to Gremlin. "I'll take him from here."

"Gremlin can carry to Home for you, yes?" Gremlin asked.

"Thanks," Blade responded. "But the Warriors will take over now." He drew his right Bowie.

Gremlin released the Russian.

Lieutenant Lysenko dropped to the ground, landing on his knees. The razor edge of a Bowie was abruptly applied to his neck.

"You give me any trouble," Blade stated, "and I'll let Hickok have you! Stand up! Move!"

Lysenko obeyed.

Blade started ushering the Russian in the direction of the Home.

"Hey!" Lynx called.

Blade paused. "What?"

"What about us?" Lynx inquired. "No 'thank you'? No pat on the back? No parade in our honor?"

"I'm sure Hickok will thank you personally," Blade said. "I appreciate what you did. You three caught up with them much faster than we could have—"

"You got that right," Lynx commented.

"—but I must get this one locked up, and see how Sherry is doing, and send out a detail for the bodies of Jean and Claudia. Talk to you later," Blade remarked. He took another step, prodding the Russian officer with his Bowie.

"What about these dead troopers?" Ferret inquired. "Want us to leave them here?"

"No," Blade replied over his right shoulder. "They might attract a mutate, or something worse. Bury them."

Lynx watched the Warrior chief and the Red disappear in the trees, then turned, gesturing angrily. "How about that? We pull Sherry's fat out of the fire, and this is the thanks we get! Bury them? I say we leave 'em for the worms!"

"Blade wants them buried," Ferret said.

"So who is he? Our fairy godmother? Why do we have to listen to him?" Lynx retorted.

"You know why," Gremlin mentioned. "The Family has been nice to us, yes? Given us a place to live, when no one else would, no? We owe them, yes?"

Lynx sighed. "Yeah, I guess we do. But I've got to tell you guys something." He placed his hands on his hips. "I'm gettin' real tired of this life. I mean, I'm bored to tears! Oh, sure, the Family is as sweet a bunch of people as you'd ever want to meet. And they've been real nice to us. Feedin' us. Treatin' us like one of their own."

"What's wrong with that?" Gremlin wanted to know. "Is pleasant, yes?"

"Yeah," Lynx agreed, "but it's also a pain in the butt! Look! We were just talkin' about the good Doktor, about how he created us to be killing machines. Well, I don't know about you two clowns, but I'm dying for some excitement in my life! Something to get the blood flowin', if you know what I mean."

"I do," Ferret said, listening attentively.

"Wasting these morons was the most fun I've had in ages," Lynx went on.

"I did . . . enjoy . . . myself," Ferret acknowledged.

"See?" Lynx said. "I'll be honest with you. The

Family is so devoted to the Spirit, so involved with loving one another and being kind and courteous and all, sometimes they make me want to puke!"

Gremlin appeared to be shocked. "You exaggerate, yes?"

"A little," Lynx confessed. "But you get my drift."

"So what can we do about it?" Ferret asked.

"There's nothing we can do, no?" Gremlin stated.

"We could leave the Home," Ferret suggested.

Gremlin's mouth dropped. "Ferret not serious, yes?"

"Why not?" Ferret countered. "I like the Family too. But there might be somewhere else in the world where we'd fit in even better."

"Gremlin never leave Home," Gremlin stated.

"Neither would I," Lynx agreed.

"But you just said—" Ferret began.

"I said," Lynx replied, cutting him off, "I was bored to tears. Not stupid! We've never had it so good. The Family are our friends. We'd be idiots to cut out on them."

"Then how do you plan to inject some excitement into your life?" Ferret inquired skeptically.

"There has to be a way," Lynx declared.

"I don't see how," Ferret said.

"Me neither," Gremlin remarked.

Lynx sighed. "Well, let's get to plantin' these jerks."

Gremlin scoured the earth for a likely spot. "Too bad we're not Warriors, yes?" he commented absently, squatting.

Lynx's ears perked up. "What? What did you say?"

Gremlin began scooping some soft dirt from a small grassy patch. "Too bad we're not Warriors, yes? Then we could do like Blade and the others, no? Lynx have more excitement than he'd know what to do with, yes?" Gremlin chuckled at the preposterous notion.

Lynx reacted as if he'd been zapped by a lightning bolt. He straightened, his eyes widening and gleaming from a dawning revelation. His hands shook with excitement. "That's it!"

"That's what?" Ferret asked.

"That's how we'll do it!" Lynx, unable to restrain his

enthusiasm, jumped up and down several times, cackling.

Ferret and Gremlin exchanged glances.

Lynx ran over to Gremlin and, before Gremlin quite knew what he was about, gave him a fleeting hug. "You did it!" he shouted in delight. "You're brilliant!"

Gremlin was flabbergasted.

"What are you babbling about?" Ferret demanded.

"Don't you see?" Lynx replied ecstatically.

"All I see," Ferret said, "is you acting like an idiot."

"You don't get it?" Lynx gazed at both of them.

"Get what?" Ferret inquired.

Lynx shook his head, grinning. "Look. I'll spell it out for you dummies! Who's responsible for the security of the Home?"

"The Warriors," Ferret answered.

"And who's pledged to protect the Family?" Lynx queried.

"The Warriors," Ferret responded.

"Exactly! And who's always gettin' involved in a fight of some kind or another in the performance of their duties?"

Ferret pursed his lips and glanced at Gremlin. "Is he leading up to what I think he's leading up to?"

Lynx smiled contentedly. "The solution is simple! If we want some excitement in our lives, some thrills to alleviate the boredom, then"—he paused—"we become Warriors!"

Ferret snorted and shook his head.

Gremlin laughed.

Lynx was offended. "What's the matter with you two? It's a great idea!"

"The only way you'll ever come up with a great idea," Ferret said, "is if you have a brain transplant."

"Very funny!" Lynx said stiffly.

"I'm not trying to hurt your feelings," Ferret stated. "But think about your proposal."

"What's wrong with it?" Lynx asked.

"Everything. For starters, the Family already has enough Warriors. Fifteen, isn't it? Divided into five Triads of three Warriors apiece. They don't need another Triad,'' Ferret said.

"How do you know?'' Lynx countered. "Plato might like the idea.''

"I'm not finished,'' Ferret remarked. "Being a Warrior isn't a post you take lightly. It's a major responsibility. All of those people are relying on you to safeguard them from harm. Their lives are in your hands.'' He paused. "It's not a job you take for the fun of it.''

Gremlin snickered.

"Who said I'd take the job lightly?'' Lynx demanded.

"Ferret is right,'' Gremlin chimed in. "Being a Warrior is very important, yes? Without Warriors, the Family would not survive in this world, no?''

"So who said I'd take it lightly?'' Lynx reiterated angrily.

"Forget it,'' Ferret suggested.

"Who died and appointed you leader?'' Lynx rejoined.

"Lynx forget it, yes?'' Gremlin said, adding his opinion.

Lynx looked from one to the other. "I'm not givin' up that easily. I'll find a way to convince you.''

"I don't take bribes,'' Ferret quipped.

Lynx's shoulders slumped dejectedly. "You know, it's true what they say.''

"What do they say?'' Ferret asked, walking over to assist Gremlin with the digging.

"Nobody really appreciates a genius,'' Lynx commented seriously.

Ferret chuckled. "Show us a genius, and we'll appreciate him.''

Gremlin stared at Lynx. "Genius help us dig, yes? Or maybe genius is too good for manual labor, no?''

Lynx vented his frustration by hissing. "Ingrates!'' he muttered.

Ferret nudged Gremlin. "If he's acting this crazy today, we'd best keep a close eye on him tonight.''

Gremlin's forehead creased. "Why?''

"The moon will be out.''

2

The Family was in an uproar by the time Blade returned to the compound. Everyone was gathered near the drawbridge, anxiously watching the Warriors and the Elders go about their business. News of the deaths of Claudia and Jean had already spread and was the main topic of discussion, along with the implications of the Soviet attack.

Blade, his prisoner in front of him, came across the drawbridge. He spotted the man he needed, a stocky Indian dressed all in green, armed with a genuine tomahawk angled through his brown belt, and an Arminius .357 revolver in a shoulder holster under his right arm. "Geronimo!" Blade called.

Geronimo shouldered his way through the throng. His brown eyes studied the Russian. "Spartacus said you wanted us to stay here until you returned," he commented.

"I'll explain everything later," Blade said. He scanned the compound. "Did Hickok make it back with Sherry?"

"Just arrived a bit ago," Geronomi replied. "Hickok wouldn't let anyone touch her. He took her to the infimary."

Blade indicated the Red soldier. "Take him there too. And don't let Hickok kill him."

"Will do." Geronimo drew the Arminius. "Let's go!" The crowd parted to permit their passage.

A diminutive man with Oriental features, dressed all in black and carrying a katana in its scabbard in his right hand, dashed up to Blade. "Orders?" he asked.

Blade sheathed his Bowie, then pointed at the forest. "Take your Triad, Rikki, and retrieve the bodies of Jean and Claudia. They're about ten to fifteen yards into the trees. You'll also find a pair of dead Russians. Strip them and bury their bodies. Bring me their belongings."

Rikki-Tikki-Tavi nodded. "We're on our way," he said, and raced off.

A tall man with his blond hair in a crew cut, wearing buckskin pants and a brown shirt, with a broadsword attached to his wide leather belt, jogged up to the head Warrior. "I kept them all back, just like you wanted," he stated.

"You did a good job, Spartacus," Blade said. "Now I want you to notify every Warrior we're on alert status. I want Gamma, Omega, and Zulu Triads on the walls within five minutes. Got that?"

"Consider it done," Spartacus responded, and left.

Blade started toward the concrete structure that housed the infirmary.

"Blade!" someone cried.

Blade turned.

It was the Family leader, Plato. His long gray hair and beard were stirred by the breeze as he approached. His wrinkled features conveyed his apprehension. He was dressed in faded jeans and a baggy blue shirt. "I need your report," he stated. "The Elders will be meeting in emergency session as soon as you provide the essential details."

"Come with me to the infirmary," Blade suggested. "I'll fill you in along the way."

Plato fell in beside Blade, and they headed in the direction of the concrete blocks.

The Home was a model of utility and conservation. The eastern half was preserved in its natural state and used for agricultural purposes. A row of log cabins for the married couples and their children occupied the middle of the 30-acre compound, extending in a line from north to south. In the western portion of the Home, grouped in a triangular configuration, were six huge concrete blocks, each designated by a letter. The Family armory was A Block, located at the southern tip of the triangle. The founder, Kurt Carpenter, had personally supervised stocking the armory with every possible weapon and insured adequate ammunition, where needed, was stockpiled. One hundred yards to the northwest of A Block was B Block, the domicile for single Family members. Another hundred yards to the northwest of B Block was the infirmary, C Block, managed by the Family Healers. An equal distance to the east of the infirmary was D Block, the spacious workshop outfitted with thousands of tools and other equipment. One hundred yards east of D Block was E Block, the gigantic Family library. Carpenter had crammed its shelves with hundreds of thousands of books, encompassing every imaginable subject. Finally, a hundred yards to the Southwest of E Block was the large building used by the Family Tillers, F Block.

"Enlighten me," Plato said.

"I was on the west wall with Hickok and Spartacus," Blade elaborated. "I'd just sent Sherry out as an escort for two new Healers."

"Yes," Plato commented. "Jean and Claudia. They were conducting their herb identification test."

"There was shooting," Blade continued. "We ran down the stairs. I found Lynx, Ferret, and Gremlin standing near the drawbridge, so I enlisted their help. Spartacus was left behind, to keep everyone back. We raced to the woods and found the bodies of two dead Russian soldiers, and"—he paused, frowning—"the bodies of the two Healers."

"What then?" Plato asked.

"I sent Lynx, Ferret, and Gremlin on ahead. They can move a lot faster than we can. They caught up with three Russians, trying to cart Sherry off. Two of the Russians were killed, but we do have an officer prisoner. That's about it," Blade succinctly concluded.

"And Sherry?"

"We'll know in a minute," Blade said.

They hurried toward C Block.

"What do you think Nathan will do if Sherry has been harmed?" Plato asked, referring to Hickok by the name his parents had bestowed upon him at birth. Each Family member, on their 16th birthday, was formally rechristened during a special Naming ceremony. Kurt Carpenter inaugurated the rite. The Founder had worried that subsequent generations might neglect their historical antecedents, might forget about the history of humankind and the factors leading up to World War Three. Carpenter had tried to insure his followers never lost touch with their roots. He had persuaded them to have their children search the history books, and when the young men and women turned 16, they were permitted to select the name of any historical figure they admired as their very own. This practice became known as the Naming, and it survived Carpenter's death. The Family expanded on it, allowing the youths to take a name from any book in the library. Compliance was not mandatory, but most members adhered to the observance. A few retained the names given them by their parents. Even fewer created a new name of their own. In every case, the name chosen was supposed to reflect the personality of its holder. Thus, 16-year-old Nathan became Hickok. The strapping Michael picked an entirely new name, predicated on his preference for edged weapons, and became known as Blade. Lone Elk became Geronimo. Clayton became Plato. And 16-year-old Chang, aspiring to achieve perfection as a martial artist and devoted to the ideal of conserving spiritual value and protecting the Family, became Rikki-Tikki-Tavi.

"I expect Hickok will declare war on the Soviets," Blade predicted.

"At least they would be evenly matched," Plato commented.

They reached the enormous concrete block and entered the front door. Only five people occupied the building. Seated on a cot to the right of the entrance was the Russian officer. Geronimo stood three feet from the cot, his .357 trained on the officer's head. Dozens of cots, aligned in two rows, filled the middle of the infirmary. Medical cabinets were dispersed at prudent intervals. On one of the cots in the center was Sherry. Beside her knelt Hickok. Standing on the far side of the cot was one of the Healers, a brown-haired woman dressed in white.

Blade walked over to Sherry's cot. "How is she, Nightingale?" he asked the Healer.

"I can answer that for you," Sherry unexpectedly

responded, and sat up. "I'm fine," she told Blade.

Hickok held up a white cloth smelling of chloroform. "Geronimo found this in one of the bastard's pockets. I reckon they wanted her alive and unhurt. Thank the Spirit!"

Sherry stared into Blade's eyes. "I let everyone down. I'm sorry."

Blade knew what she meant. "You were ambushed and outnumbered. There was no way you could have prevented the deaths of Jean and Claudia."

Sherry frowned, her profound inner turmoil evident. "Yes, there was," she said slowly. "I sensed something was wrong. I should have acted differently."

"Believe me," Blade assured her. "No one will blame you for what happened."

Sherry's green eyes mirrored her emotional agony as she replied. "Yes, there is someone. Me."

Hickok glanced up at Blade, his mouth downturned.

"I need to interrogate the Russian," Blade said. "But I want to talk with you about this later. All right?" he queried Sherry.

Sherry nodded. "I'll come see you," she promised.

Blade smiled encouragingly, then turned, Plato still at his side.

"Sherry is adversely affected by her experience," Plato commented when they were beyond hearing range.

"I know," Blade agreed. "We've both seen the same symptoms many times before. If she doesn't conquer her doubt, if she doesn't realize she didn't fail in her duty, she'll be washed up as a Warrior."

"Curious, isn't it?" Plato thoughtfully remarked. "A Warrior can be in superb physical condition, can be supremely skilled with a variety of weapons and in hand-to-hand combat, and yet, if the Warriors lacks the proper mental attitude, all the conditioning and skill in the world are wasted."

Blade nodded. They were nearing the Russian's cot. The officer was glaring at them. This one wasn't going to be easy to crack. Drastic measures were called for. "Has he given you any trouble?" Blade asked

Geronimo as they reached the cot.

"He's been a good little boy," Geronimo answered. "From the way he's been squirming, I think he needs to go potty."

"Is that right?" Blade asked. "Would you like to relieve yourself?"

The officer nodded.

"Tough," Blade snapped, and before anyone could gauge his intent, before Plato could hope to stop him, he lashed out with his right fist, catching the officer in the mouth and sending him head over heels from the cot.

"Blade!" Plato yelled.

Blade stepped over the cot and reached the officer while the Russian was still on his knees. He flicked his right foot up and out, connecting, slamming his instep into the Russian's ribs, knocking the officer onto his back.

"Blade! Stop!" Plato cried.

Blade's left hand grabbed the gasping officer under the chin. He squeezed and lifted, his arm bulging, hauling the Russian from the cement floor and into the air.

Plato went to grip Blade's arm, but Geronimo quickly stepped between them, shaking his head.

Blade drew his right Bowie and pressed the tip into the Russian's genitals.

The officer squirmed and thrashed, wheezing, his eyes bulging.

"Now that I've managed to stimulate your interest," Blade said, "I'm going to tell you how it is." He paused, his gray eyes boring into the officer's. "You killed two of my Family, you son of a bitch! I'd end your murderous career right now, but I need information. So here's how it is. I'm going to ask you some questions. If you refuse to answer them, you're dead. If you hesitate, you're dead. If I suspect you're lying, you're dead. You can tough it out and die, or you can cooperate and live. If you follow me so far, nod."

The officer nodded. Vigorously.

"Good. I want you to think about something. If you

refuse to answer, if you value loyalty more than your life, no one is ever going to know how brave you were! Your buddies, your comrades, will never know how you died! You'll have died in vain! Think about it. And about this. If you cooperate, I'll give you a canteen and some jerky and let you go. My word on it. We've released prisoners before. We're not butchers, like you. We don't kill innocent women. But, as the Spirit is my witness, I will gut you like a fish if you don't give me the answers I need." Blade unceremoniously dumped the Russian on the cot.

The officer landed on his left side. He coughed and sputtered, rubbing his neck, gaping at the giant Warrior.

Blade held the right Bowie out, slowly moving his wrist back and forth, allowing the light to gleam off the blade. "What's your name?"

"Lysenko," the officer instantly replied. "Lieutenant Frol Lysenko."

"Why were you sent here?" Blade demanded.

"To capture one of your Family alive and transport them to Washington," Lysenko responded.

"How were you going to get back?" Blade asked.

"By helicopter," Lysenko said.

Blade pondered a moment. "Is this helicopter waiting for you or are you supposed to signal it?"

"Signal," Lysenko disclosed.

"How are you to signal it?" Blade queried. "Be specific."

"We have a portable radio transmitter stashed about ten miles southeast of here," Lysenko answered.

Blade contemplated his next question. He was excited about the transmitter. If the radio could be retrieved, the Family would be able to monitor the Soviet broadcasts and perhaps learn information crucial to the continued safety of the Freedom Federation. "How did you discover the location of the Home?"

Lysenko almost laughed. He hesitated for a fraction, then recoiled in fear as the Bowie slashed toward his abdomen. "The spy!" he screamed. "The spy!"

Blade halted his stroke inches from Lysenko's

stomach. His brow creased. "Spy? What spy?"

"We have a spy stationed in Denver," Lysenko revealed.

Blade straightened. A spy in Denver? In the capital of the Civilized Zone, one of the Family's allies? "What's the name of this spy?"

"I don't know," Lysenko said. He saw Blade's arm tense. "Honest! I really don't! General Malenkov never told me. All I know is a spy infiltrated the government of President Toland about a month ago, and has been feeding us classified information ever since."

Blade and Plato exchanged glances. President Toland was the duly elected leader of the Civilized Zone, and one of the few people aware of the Home's *exact* location. Many persons knew the Home was in Minnesota, but Minnesota contained almost 80,000 square miles. Anyone searching for the compound could waste a decade in the hunt and still come up empty.

"You mentioned General Malenkov," Blade noted. "Is this the same Malenkov Hickok encountered when he was in Washington, D.C.?"

Lysenko nodded. "Hickok's escape embarrassed the general. It was so public . . . so spectacular. And so many lives were lost! The general hates your Family. He wants you eliminated."

Blade nearly grinned. General Malenkov's reaction was understandable. Hickok, with his usual flair for mayhem, had stirred up the proverbial hornet's nest in the former American capital. "All right. You stay put. I'll be back to question you some more later." He glanced at Geronimo. "Escort him to the bathroom. Then park him here until further notice."

"You've got it," Geronimo said.

Blade looked at Plato, then nodded toward the doorway.

Plato followed the Warrior chief outside into the bright sunlight.

"Is there anything you want me to ask him?" Blade inquired.

"Not offhand," Plato said. "We are already familiar

with the Soviet system, and cognizant of their logistical and industrial problems, thanks to Nathan." He paused. "We must contact Toland and inform him about the spy. Perhaps this secret agent can be apprehended." He paused again, frowning. "But there is something I would like to discuss with you."

"What is it?"

"Before I proceed," Plato stated, "I must qualify my complaint." He adopted a paternal air. "Blade, I know the Founder had his reasons for organizing the Family the way it is. I know Carpenter believed it was necessary for the head of the Warriors to be permitted to override the Family Leader in a time of crisis. I comprehend the wisdom of the arrangement. And I know interrogating a prisoner is your province." Plato sighed. "But I really must protest your treatment of Lieutenant Lysenko."

Blade went to speak, but Plato held up his hand.

"Bear with me," Plato said. "Lysenko isn't the first prisoner you have treated so brutally. I doubt he will be the last. And, yes, I can recognize the validity of the psychology behind your methods. But I want to pose a moral issue for your consideration. Don't answer me right away. Meditate on this." He cleared his throat. "We, the Family, believe in the guidance of the Spirit in our lives. We believe in exalted concepts of love and brotherhood, don't we?"

"Yes," Blade replied.

"We are, after a fashion, symbols for those still languishing in a squalid cultural darkness, are we not?"

"I never thought of it that way," Blade admitted.

"You should," Plato said. "Talk to some of your friends in the Freedom Federation. You'll be surprised at how favorably they view our accomplishments."

"What's this have to do with my methods?" Blade asked.

"Simply this. If we claim to be living on a higher moral and spiritual plane than those unfortunates still suffering from the delayed ravages of the nuclear war, don't we have a certain responsibility to them and ourselves to conduct our behavior according to our highest spiritual dictates?"

Blade studied his mentor. He'd always admired Plato's wisdom, and reciprocated Plato's abiding affection. But in this instance, he felt, the Family Leader was wrong. "So what you're getting at," he deduced, "is that I should treat our prisoners differently. Not be as hard on them. Is that it?"

"Precisely," Plato said, smiling. "You see my point?"

"I see it," Blade declared.

"Excellent."

"But I don't agree," Blade commented.

"Why not?"

Blade raised his right hand and pointed at the west wall. "On the other side of that wall is a world filled with evil, a world where people are murdered over trifles, a world where survival of the fittest is the norm. Oh, there are a few exceptions. The Civilized Zone. The Flathead Indians. The Cavalry. Us. But by and large, a lot of folks out there take each day as it comes, never knowing if they'll still be alive at the end of it or not. There's no peace of mind, no security. Existence is hand to mouth." He swept the compound with his hand. "Well, that's never going to happen *here!* I won't allow it! The only reason we're able to live on a higher moral and spiritual plane, as you put it, is because those walls, and the Warriors, keep all the killers, all of the degenerates, all of the power-mongers, and every other type of social parasite conceivable *outside* the Home. Not everybody lives on the same plane we do. A lot of people are outright evil. Wicked. Living to harm others." Blade leaned toward Plato. "The only methods those vermin understand are the same methods they employ. Violence. And more violence. And if that's what it takes to preserve the Family, then those are the methods I'll employ!"

This time it was Plato's turn to open his mouth to speak; instead, he mutely scrutinized his protegé. Plato had taken Blade under his wing after the death of Blade's father, had even let it be known he wanted Blade to succeed him as Family Leader after his demise. He knew Blade was an outstanding Warrior, perhaps the best the Family had ever seen. Oh, Blade wasn't as deadly as, say Hickok or Rikki or Yama. But Blade's overall temperament, despite his tendency to brood periodically, qualified him to be the top Warrior. One day, Plato hoped, if his tutelage was successful, Blade would also qualify to hold the post of Family Leader.

Blade gently placed his right hand on Plato's left shoulder. "I'm sorry if my methods disturb you. But it simply can't be helped." He somberly gazed at the west wall. "You haven't been out there, Plato. You haven't seen what it's like. The constant killing, the senseless slaughter. You must stay on your guard from the moment you leave the Home until the moment you step back inside. It's sheer hell."

"True, I haven't journeyed beyond the Home as extensively as you have," Plato acknowledged. "But I'm not naive either. I've survived attacks by a variety of mutations, the clouds, and wild animals. I saw the carnage the Trolls wrought when they invaded the Home and abducted some of our dearest friends and loved ones. If you'll recall, I readily assented to sending Alpha Triad to Fox to save the kidnapped women. I also lived through an all-out assault by the Civilized Zone Army while you were in Denver. I wasn't born yesterday. I know the postwar era is rife with bloodshed, and violence rules. I only wish we didn't need to subscribe to it."

"We have no choice," Blade stated.

Plato sighed wistfully. "I'm reluctant to admit it, but apparently you're right. It's so distressing, though, to see us pulled down to their level."

"When dealing with trash," Blade philosophized, "you have to expect to get a little dirty."

Plato scrunched up his nose. "I wish you wouldn't define it in quite those terms."

"Just thank the Spirit there's a big difference between them and us," Blade mentioned.

"Which difference do you mean?" Plato inquired.

"We may slip into the muck now and then," Blade said. "But at least we can climb out again." He paused. "Bastards like Lysenko, and the Trolls and the Doktor too, live in it. Wallow in it. Enjoy it."

Plato deliberated for a minute. "I never considered the matter in that light."

"Try it sometime," Blade recommended. "You'll sleep better at night."

3

Morning of the next day.

Six men and a woman were gathered near the open drawbridge in the west wall of the Home. Lieutenant Lysenko stood meekly in the middle of the group. The gunfighter, Hickok, was to his right. The Indian, Geronimo, to his left. Three other Warriors ringed him. One of them, a tall blond man in buckskin pants and a green shirt, armed with a broadsword, was familiar. Lysenko had seen Blade conversing with the man the day before in the infirmary, after Blade had returned to continue his interrogation. The Warrior with the broadsword was named Spartacus. But the other two were new to Lysenko.

One was a beautiful dusky woman with an Afro. She wore a green fatigue shirt and pants, black boots, and carried an M-16. For some mysterious reason, she couldn't seem to keep her eyes off Hickok.

The other newcomer was a youth, obviously shy of his 20th birthday, possibly even younger. His hair and eyes were brown, his eyebrows bushy. Whether deliberately or not, he wore his long hair in the same style as Hickok. His clothing was all black, and patterned after a cut Lysenko was unfamiliar with, incorporating wide lapels and tight pants legs. A revolver was strapped to his right thigh.

Blade was four feet away, arms at his side, glancing from one to the other. "You have your instructions. Any questions?"

"Yeah," Hickok said. He grinned at Lysenko. "If

this cow chip makes a break for it, can I perforate his noggin?"

"Do whatever is necessary," Blade advised, "but keep him alive until after you retrieve the radio transmitter. I don't care what happens to him afterwards."

Lysenko frowned. "You promised I would be set free if I helped you!" he protested.

"And you will be," Blade assured him.

Lysenko nodded toward Hickok. "How do I know he will do as you say? How do I know he won't decide to kill me on the way back?"

"Hickok is a Warrior," Blade stated. "He follows orders."

Hickok leaned toward the officer, smirking. "Which makes you the luckiest hombre alive."

"It's only ten miles there, and ten back," Blade addressed them. "I expect you here before dark."

"No problem," Geronimo said. In addition to his tomahawk and the Arminius, he carried a Marlin 45-70.

Blade glanced at Hickok. "All of you should take rifles or automatics," he commented.

Hickok nodded, then looked at the youth in black. "Shane, I want you to run to the armory and grab a rifle or whatever, and pick one up for Spartacus."

"I prefer a Heckler and Koch HK93," Spartacus said to Shane.

Shane started to run off.

"Whoa!" Hickok called.

Shane stopped and turned.

"Swing by my cabin, will you, and ask Sherry for my Henry?" Hickok said, referring to his cherished Navy Arms Henry Carbine.

Shane grinned, eager to please his acknowledged hero. "I'll be back in a jiffy," he promised, and sprinted to the east.

The black woman laughed. "That boy'd lick your boots clean if you asked him!"

"I'm not wearing boots," Hickok rejoined.

"Moccasins. Boots." The black woman shrugged. "It wouldn't make no nevermind to Shane. Ain't you noticed how he's put you up on a pedestal?"

"I've noticed, Bertha," Hickok said, sighing.

"Shane isn't the only one," Geronimo interjected, winking at Bertha.

"And what's that supposed to mean?" Bertha demanded.

"Oh, nothing," Geronimo responded, grinning mischievously.

Blade smiled. Bertha's long-standing crush on Hickok was common gossip around the Home. She'd been interested in the gunman ever since they'd met in Thief River Falls. Even Hickok's later marriage to Sherry hadn't dampened Bertha's ardor. Although she was regularly seen in the company of several Family men, Bertha had never taken a mate. Some said she was holding out, saving herself in the forlorn hope Hickok might one day become available. Hickok, Blade knew, was extremely uncomfortable over the situation, but didn't seem to know what to do about it. Sherry appeared to tolerate Bertha's affection for her husband, as long as the affection was kept at a distance.

There was a sudden commotion to the north.

Blade looked to his right, puzzled. There they were. At it again. Lynx, Ferret, and Gremlin. The trio had spent every waking moment since their return yesterday, arguing. He couldn't imagine the cause of their dispute, but it was evident Lynx was constantly remonstrating with the other two over something.

"I'll be back in a bit, pard," Hickok declared, and walked toward the bickering mutants. He could see Ferret and Gremlin shaking their heads, and Lynx gesturing angrily. A few of the words Lynx was saying became audible.

" . . . morons . . . couldn't find your butts . . . broad daylight . . . !"

Ferret spotted the gunman when he was still ten yards off, and quickly whispered to the other two.

The argument abruptly ceased.

Hickok chuckled as he neared them.

All three faced the gunfighter. All three were smiling serenely. All three smiles were patently phony.

"What's with you bozos?" Hickok greeted them.

"You've been spattin' like three stallions over a mare on the make!"

Lynx stretched his fake grin even wider. "Spattin'? Us? No way. We've been havin' an intelligent discussion."

Ferret snorted.

Lynx ignored him. "What can we do for you, Hickok?"

Hickok stared at each of them. "I plumb forgot yesterday. I owe you boys a debt."

"No, you don't," Lynx said.

"You saved my missus from those pricks," Hickok stated. "I wanted to thank each of you, personal-like. And let you know I'm in your debt. If there's ever anything I can do for you, just say the word."

"There's no need," Lynx declared.

"Yes, there is," Hickok disagreed.

"You're our friend," Lynx elaborated. "You've always treated us with respect. We just returned the favor."

Hickok put his right hand on Lynx's shoulder. "I'm serious about this. I'll never be able to thank you enough. Anything I can do for you, I will."

"Thanks," Lynx said, "but you don't . . ." He stopped, blinking rapidly.

"What's wrong?" Hickok asked.

"Nothin'," Lynx replied, beginning to smile again.

"I'll be seein' you," Hickok said, and began to turn away.

"Just a minute!" Lynx said, a look of triumph on his face.

Hickok paused. "What is it?"

"Can you clarify somethin' for me?" Lynx inquired.

"If I can" Hickok answered. "Shoot."

Lynx beamed at Ferret and Gremlin, then faced the gunman. "I need some info about the Warriors."

"What about them?" Hickok replied.

"To become a candidate for consideration by the Elders," Lynx said, "doesn't a person have to be nominated by a Warrior?"

"Uh-oh," Ferret interjected.

Hickok glanced at Ferret, perplexed, then answered Lynx. "We call it being sponsored. A candidate for Warrior status must be sponsored by an active Warrior before the Elders will vote on admittin' them to the Warrior ranks. Why?"

"Oh, just curious," Lynx lied. "Tell me somethin'. How many candidates can a single Warrior sponsor?"

"I don't follow you," Hickok said.

"For instance," Lynx detailed, "let's pretend two people want to become Warriors. Could a single Warrior, like yourself for example, sponsor both of them?"

Hickok pondered for a moment. "It's never been done that way before, but I reckon it would be okay."

"And what about if three people wanted to become Warriors," Lynx went on. "Could you sponsor all three?"

"I could give it a shot," Hickok said. "And I could always talk Blade, Geronimo, or one of the others into sidin' with me. Why?"

"No reason," Lynx stated. "Like I said. I was just curious."

"Are you thinkin' of becoming a Warrior?" Hickok asked.

"No, he isn't!" Ferret responded before Lynx could answer.

"Must excuse Lynx, yes?" Gremlin added. "Received bump on head yesterday, no?"

"I did not!" Lynx declared testily.

Hickok saw Shane racing from the east, his arms laden with the requested weapons. "I'll be seein' you," he told them.

"I'd like to talk to you when you get back," Lynx said.

"No, he wouldn't," Ferret remarked.

Hickok shook his head and ambled toward the drawbridge. Behind him, Lynx, Ferret, and Gremlin started up again in hushed tones.

" . . . idiots!" Lynx snapped.

" . . . not asking him!" Ferret responded.

Hickok could only distinguish a few more words as he

moved away.

" . . . had a brain . . . be dangerous!" came from Lynx.

" . . . over my dead body!" came from Ferret.

". . . be arranged!" was part of Lynx's rejoinder.

And then Hickok was out of hearing range. He wondered if Lynx did, indeed, want to become a Warrior. Hickok favored the notion. He'd seen Lynx in action during the Battle of Armageddon, as the Family liked to call the fight in Catlow, Wyoming, and he judged Lynx to be prime Warrior material. If the runt wanted sponsorin', he'd be right proud to oblige.

"Here you go!" Shane exclaimed, out of breath, holding the guns in his arms.

Spartacus took his HK93.

Hickok grabbed his Henry.

Shane was left with a Winchester Model 94 and his Llama Comanche .357 Magnum on his right hip.

Blade was standing next to Spartacus. "What was that all about?" he asked Hickok, while nodding toward the trio still debating to the north.

"Beats me, pard," Hickok admitted. "I think Lynx wants to become a Warrior, but Ferret and Gremlin don't cotton to the idea."

"Lynx a Warrior?" Blade said thoughtfully. "That's a good idea. Come to think of it, all three of them would make great Warriors."

"Maybe you should let them know," Hickok suggested.

"I'll talk to them when I get the chance," Blade said. "Right now I must find Plato." He surveyed their group. "Take care out there. May the Spirit be with you." He departed.

Hickok waved his right arm toward the drawbridge. "Let's move out! Spartacus, take the point. Shane and Bertha—the rear. Stay in sight at all times!"

The Warriors assumed their formation, and their retrieval party departed the Home. Some of the Family members ceased their activities to watch the group leave.

"You said to the southeast, right?" Hickok asked

Lysenko.

Lysenko nodded.

"Spartacus!" Hickok yelled. "Bear southeast. We'll guide you with hand signals. Stay alert!"

Spartacus nodded, moving to a position 15 yards in front of Hickok, Geronimo, and Lysenko. Bertha and Shane were an equal distance behind them.

"I hope I can find the clearing again," Lysenko commented as they crossed the field to the south of the compound.

Hickok wagged the Henry barrel in the Russian's face. "You'd best find it, you four-flushin' coyote!"

Lysenko glanced at Geronimo. "Excuse me. Is it permissible to ask you a few questions?"

"Why are you asking me?" Geronimo replied.

Lysenko motioned to Hickok. "I know he would not talk to me."

"You're not as dumb as you look," Hickok stated crisply.

Geronimo nodded. "I guess it would be all right. Blade says you've been cooperating fully with us. What do you want to know?"

"Several things," Lysenko said. "For starters, why does Hickok talk so strangely?"

Geronimo laughed. "Everybody asks the same thing. Have you ever heard of the Wild West?"

"The Old American West?" Lysenko said. "I read a little about it in one of my history classes. As you probably know, we are versed in both cultures. We study Russian and American history. And we become bilingual, speaking English and Russian fluently."

"So Hickok told us after his visit to Washington," Geronimo stated.

"Hickok talks the way he does because he likes the Old West?" Lysenko queried.

"Because he admires a man who lived way back then," Geronimo explained. "A man by the name of James Butler Hickok. The dummy in the buckskins talks the way he thinks the real Hickok would have talked."

"Most peculiar," Lysenko remarked.

"I've been saying that for years," Geronimo quipped, and laughed.

Hickok ignored them. They reached the edge of the forest and entered the trees.

"Some other aspects of your Family puzzle me," Lysenko said.

"Like what?" Geronimo responded.

"Your informal attitude, for one thing," Lynsenko stated. "You are all so relaxed in your relations. Plato is your Leader, yet not once did I observe anyone accord him any special respect. And you Warriors! Blade is your chief, yet you talk to him like you would anyone else. There is no saluting, no drill, no regimentation in your Warrior organization. You don't even wear uniforms!" he marveled.

"Why should we?" Geronimo replied.

"Regimentation promotes discipline," Lysenko commented.

"No," Geronimo corrected him, "regimentation promotes subservience. We deliberately shun formality. Our Founder was a wise man. He saw what happened to the prewar society. Everyone was required to fit into a certain mold. Behave in an acceptable manner. Wear fashionable clothes. Even trim their hair in faddish styles. If they didn't, they were considered outcasts or weird. People were denied the opportunity to express themselves, to assert their individual personality. They were manipulated by the power-mongers at every turn." He paused. "Carpenter wanted to discourage formality, so he instituted a policy allowing Family members one name, and one name only. No Mr. So-and-So. No Miss or Ms. or Mrs. He thought last names bred a sense of false civility. And he felt the same way about titles. Titles were used to make people inferior to the one with the title. There was 'Mr. President,' or 'Your Honor,' or 'Your Majesty.' Carpenter despised that practice, so he implemented a policy where each and every Family member receives a title. Whether it's Tiller, Healer, Empath, Warrior, or whatever, we're all equal socially. No one lords it over anyone else. And that's the way we prefer it."

"Amazing," Lysenko mentioned.

Hickok abruptly stopped and glared at Geronimo.

"What's wrong with you?" Geronimo asked.

"Why the blazes are you being so nice to this prick?" Hickok demanded.

"What's the harm in a little conversation?" Geronimo retorted.

Hickok stabbed his right thumb toward Lysenko. "This bastard killed two of our sisters!"

"I know that," Geronimo said slowly.

"Then how the hell can you be so friendly toward him?" Hickok queried angrily.

"Just because I'm talking to the man doesn't make me his friend!" Geronimo stated defensively.

"It does in my book!" Hickok snapped, and marched several feet ahead.

They walked in an uncomfortable silence for several minutes.

"I know it's not any consolation," Lysenko said in a restrained voice, "but I deeply regret what happened to the two women."

"Sure you do, you mangy varmint!" Hickok barked over his left shoulder.

"I do!" Lysenko insisted. "I was merely following orders—and I know that's no excuse—and I see that it was wrong."

Hickok snorted.

Lysenko glanced at the stocky Indian. "You believe me, don't you?"

Geronimo laughed. "Doesn't matter what I believe."

"But I'm sincere!" Lysenko said. "I've never felt like this before. Never felt remorse over the slaying of an enemy."

"Enemy!" Hickok exploded, whirling. "They were Healers, you Red scum! They were devoted to helpin' others! They wanted to relieve suffering and pain! And you and your rotten henchmen killed 'em!"

Lysenko blanched.

Hickok's right hand dropped near his right Python. "Not another word out of you, you hear? Don't speak unless you're spoken to! You got that?"

Lysenko nodded.

Hickok wheeled and stalked off.

Geronimo studied the broad back of his best friend, worried. He had never seen Hickok so emotional over the death of a Family member, or in this case two, before. The gunman was hotheaded at times, even reckless on occasion. But he rarely permitted his feelings to impair his better judgment. So why was Hickok acting so temperamentally now? Was it because Sherry had nearly been abducted? Was Hickok regretting having agreed to Sherry becoming a Warrior? Or was it something else? Hickok had loved another woman before Sherry, a Warrior named Joan. Joan had been slain in the line of duty, despite Hickok's efforts to protect her from harm. Had the unsettling incident with Sherry and the Russians rekindled his anxiety? Was the gunman tormented by the prospect of losing Sherry too? Geronimo increased his speed, caught up with his friend.

"What do you want?" Hickok barked. "Why don't you stick with your Commie buddy?"

Geronimo's brown eyes narrowed. "That crack was uncalled for, and you damn well know it!"

Hickok didn't reply.

"Nathan," Geronimo said, "I'm sorry."

"You should be!" Hickok said.

"Not for talking to Lysenko," Geronimo stated. "You know as well as I why I did it."

"Oh? Do I?" Hickok rejoined acidly.

"Yeah. We covered it in our Warrior Psychology Class, remember? How if you engage an enemy in idle chitchat, sometimes they'll let an important fact slip without realizing it," Geronimo elaborated.

"Whoop-de-do for psychology!" Hickok commented.

Geronimo frowned. "Cut the crap and listen to me! I said I was sorry. Not about Lysenko. But about you."

"Me?"

"Yeah, dimwit. I should have realized sooner how upset you were about Sherry. I should have been more sensitive to the hurt you're feeling inside. For that, I'm sorry," Geronimo declared.

Hickok glanced at the man who knew him better than anyone else, except perhaps Blade. His blue eyes were troubled. "I almost lost her!" he exclaimed in a tortured whisper.

"But you didn't," Geronimo reminded him.

"I would have," Hickok said, "if it hadn't been for Lynx and the others. They could trail the Russians by scent, and do in minutes what would have taken us hours tryin' to find tracks." He paused, then visibly shivered. "I almost lost her, Geronimo!"

"Don't be so hard on yourself," Geronimo advised. "It wasn't your fault."

"You know," Hickok said softly, for once neglecting to use his Wild West jargon, "I don't know if I could stand to have it happen again. Losing Joan was terrible, the worst experience in my life. When Sherry first told me she wanted to become a Warrior, I really came close to telling her we were through if she did. But I decided I couldn't put a leash on her, couldn't make her live the kind of life I figured was right for her. She has a mind of her own. She can make her own decisions."

"I think you did the right thing," Geronimo remarked.

"I thought so too," Hickok concurred. "But now I'm not so sure." He stared into Geronimo's eyes. "If I lose her, I don't know what I'll do."

"Why worry about it?" Geronimo asked. "Like you said, Sherry has a mind of her own. You couldn't have stopped her from becoming a Warrior, even if you wanted to. The best you can do now is to hang in there, to be there when she needs you, and pray nothing happens to her."

"I reckon you're right," Hickok observed. He exhaled noisily. "Danged contrary females!"

"Look!" Geronimo suddenly exclaimed, pointing directly ahead.

Hickok looked.

Spartacus was hiding behind a tree trunk, motioning for them to take cover.

Hickok whirled. He saw Bertha and Shane, about 15 yards off, watching him intently. He waved for them to go to ground.

Geronimo grabbed Lysenko's right arm and pulled the officer around a dense bush.

Hickok spotted a low boulder five yards to his left. He ran to the rock and crouched. What in the blazes was it? he wondered. He cradled the Henry and peered over the top of the boulder.

Just in time.

The cause of Spartacus's alarm plodded into view. Once, the monstrosity might have been a whitetail buck, hardly a menace to humans. But now the hapless buck had been transformed, changed into a hairless, pus-covered horror by the regenerating chemical clouds, one of the many biological-warfare elements employed during World War Three. Ordinary mammals, reptiles, and amphibians could undergo the same revolting metamorphosis. Hair and scales would fall off, and be replaced by blistering sores. Green mucus would spew from their ears and nose. Their teeth would yellow and rot. And they would become rabid engines of destruction, existing only to kill every living thing in their path.

The buck had stopped ten yards from Spartacus's tree loudly sniffing the air.

Hickok hoped the critter wouldn't detect their scent. This buck sported a huge rack, six points on one side alone, more than enough to inflict a fatal wound. And he knew the mutate would charge at the slightest provocation.

The Family employed different, but similar, terms to describe the various mutations proliferating since the Big Blast, as they called World War Three. The pus-covered chemically spawned creatures were known as mutates. The mutations resulting from the massive amount of radiation unleashed on the environment, producing aberrations like two-headed wolves and snakes with nine eyes, were simply labeled mutants. Insects were subject to inexplicable strains of giantism. And, finally, there were the scientifically manufactured mutations, the genetically engineered deviations. The nefarious Doktor had been responsible for Lynx, Ferret, and Gremlin, and a horde just like them. But the Doktor hadn't been the only one to tamper with nature. Hickok had read books in the Family library, books detailing the experiments conducted by dozens of scientists shortly before the Big Blast. Experiments intended to create new life forms. Better life forms. They hadn't always worked as designed. Hickok remembered reading about one such experiment in particular, one conducted in a laboratory in New York City. The genetic engineers had endeavored to bring into being a superior chimpanzee by fusing a chimp and human embryo; the resultant insane deviate had murdered 14 innocent people before it was brought to bay. The gunman ruminated on all of this as the mutate advanced several steps in his direction, still sniffing the air.

Spartacus was flat against the trunk of the tree.

The buck was now five yards from the tree, eyeing the surrounding vegetation.

Hickok glanced over his right shoulder, but he couldn't see any sign of Bertha and Shane. Perfect! The mutate would wander off if they stayed concealed.

Someone sneezed.

The sound emanated from behind the bush screening Geronimo and Lysenko.

Instantly, the mutate bounded toward the bush.

Geronimo stepped into sight, his Marlin 45-70 pressed against his shoulder, and the big gun boomed while the mutate was in midair.

The mutate was struck in the left shoulder, pus and skin spraying in every direction. The impact of the 45-70 twisted the mutate to the left, deflecting it from its course, and it landed on all fours, tensing for another leap at the human in green. But it was now two yards to the left of Spartacus's tree, in a clear line of fire.

Hickok rose up from behind the bounder, his Henry thundering, once, twice, three times in all, and each shot rocked the mutate as it was hit in the side.

Spartacus joined in with his HK93, the automatic chattering, the slugs ripping the mutate from its tail to its neck.

The mutate trembled as it was blasted again and again, uttering a harsh gurgling sound as it sank to its knees. The firing stopped.

That's when Shane dashed up to the mutate and jammed the barrel of his Winchester into its left eye. He squeezed the trigger, and the mutate's brains and an ample quantity of pus and mucus blew out the right side of its head.

The mutate dropped to the ground.

In the ensuring quiet, someone sneezed again.

Lieutenant Lysenko walked around the bush, the fingers of his right hand pinching his nose.

Hickok stepped up to the Russian. "What the blazes were you doin'? Tryin' to get us killed?"

Lysenko removed his fingers from his nose. "Sorry."

"Sorry don't make it, polecat!" Hickok said.

"I tried to prevent it," Lysenko stated.

"If it happens again," Hickok assured him, "you won't have a nose left to sneeze with!" He spun. "Let's move out!"

Geronimo fell in beside the Russian as they resumed their trek.

Lysenko looked over his right shoulder at the dead mutate. "I've heard of them, but I've never seen one before. They're horrible!"

"My Family calls them mutates," Geronimo noted. "They're all over the forest."

"We've cleared any mutations out of the cities and towns," Lysenko revealed. "But we still receive reports of them from the rural areas."

"Yep. They're all over," Geronimo reiterated. "I hope you can run fast."

Lysenko glanced at the Indian. "Why do you say that?"

"Blade's planning to release you after we retrieve the transmitter, isn't he?" Geronimo innocently asked.

"Yes," Lysenko replied slowly.

"And he'll supply you with a canteen and some jerky, right?" Geronimo said.

"Yes. So?"

"So a canteen isn't much of a weapon when it comes to facing a mutate, or any of the other . . . things . . . in the woods," Geronimo declared, suppressing a grin.

Lieutenant Lysenko stared at the trees and brush

around them. His forehead furrowed and he chewed on his lower lip. "Surely Blade will allow me to take a firearm," he said hopefully.

"Nope." Geronimo shook his head. "Sorry. But it's not our policy to arm our enemies. We've taken prisoners before, and we've always let the ones leave who wanted to leave. We've supplied them with a canteen and jerky, enough for a couple of days." Geronimo deliberately pretended to be distracted by a starling winging overhead. He feigned a yawn. "Funny, though."

"What is?" Lysenko immediately inquired.

"We don't think any of them ever made it to civilization," Geronimo mentioned.

"How would you know that?" Lysenko asked.

"We've followed a few of their tracks," Geronimo fibbed.

Lysenko leaned forward. "And?" he goaded the Warrior.

"And they just up and vanished into thin air," Geronimo said guilelessly.

Lieutenant Lysenko frowned.

"Oh! Wait!" Geronimo exclaimed.

"What?" Lysenko prompted.

"There was one we found. Well kind of. All we located was his torn, bloody shirt." Geronimo looked away so the Russian couldn't behold the twinkle in his eyes.

Lieutenant Lysenko began chewing on his lower lip in earnest.

4

"You wanted to talk to me?" Blade asked.

"Yes," Lieutenant Lysenko said, sounding irritated.

The retrieval party had returned at dusk with the radio transmitter. They had reached the clearing, found the radio, and returned without mishap. Once, in the distance, they'd seen a huge . . . thing . . . moving through the trees, but it hadn't seen them. Hickok, following Blade's instructions, had carted the radio to Plato's cabin. Spartacus, Shane, and Bertha had gone to B Block for their evening meal. Geronimo, with Lysenko in tow, had found Blade in the open area between the blocks and informed the Warrior chief that the Russian "wants a few words with you." Now, Geronimo stood eight feet away, his hands folded behind his back, whistling.

"What about?" Blade inquired.

"You know damn well what about!" Lysenko snapped. "Did you really think you'd get away with it?"

Blade, completely mystified, glanced at Geronimo. He noticed Geronimo seemed to be on the verge of laughing aloud. "Get away with what?"

"Don't play innocent with me!" Lysenko said. "I know all about it! Geronimo gave it away!"

"Oh, he did, did he?" Blade replied.

"Yes! And I'm telling you now that I won't leave here without a weapon!" Lysenko declared.

"Is that so?"

Lysenko mustered the courage to square his shoulders and face up to the giant Warrior. "Yes! I cooperated with you, didn't I? I led your people to the transmitter, didn't I?"

"Yes," Blade conceded.

"Then how can you send me out there to die?" Lysenko queried belligerently. "I know you said you've give me a canteen and jerky, but that's not enough! I've seen what's out there! I wouldn't last two days without a weapon!"

"I don't know . . ." Blade said.

"You don't have to give me one of your weapons," Lysenko stated. "Just hand over one of the AK-47's my men and I brought here."

Blade raised his right hand and scratched his chin.

"Listen!" Lysenko said, lowering his voice and inching closer to the Warrior. "Would you give me one of the AK-47's if I provided you with some classified information? How about it? The information in exchange for an AK-47?"

"What information could you possibly have?" Blade remarked disinterestedly.

"Something important," Lysenko answered.

"We already know General Malenkov wants us dead," Blade said. "And you've told us all you know about the spy in Denver. Unless"—his eyes narrowed—"you were holding back on us."

"No! I told you the truth about the spy!" Lysenko declared. "This is something else. Something of possible value to you and the entire Freedom Federation!"

"I'll listen to it," Blade stated.

"And do I get an AK-47?" Lysenko asked eagerly.

Blade sighed. "Tell you what I'll do. If the information is of value to the Freedom Federation, you'll get an AK-47 and all the ammunition you can carry. But if it isn't . . ." He let the sentence trail off.

"It will be!" Lysenko promised. He glanced around, then looked at Blade. "We were attacked."

"Attacked? By who? The Southerners?"

"No!" Lysenko responded, scoffing. "Not the wretched Rebels!"

"Then who attacked you?"

The Vikings!" Lysenko whispered.

"The what?" Blade replied skeptically.

"Hear me out," Lysenko said. "Two weeks ago Philadelphia was attacked. As you undoubtedly know, Philadelphia is under our control. It wasn't razed during the war like New York City. Our naval forces established a beachhead at Philadelphia at the outset of the war, and it was spared a nuclear strike. There are two million people residing there now. We have a major training center there for our officer corps. It's one of the few cities on the East Coast still resembling the kinds of cities they had before the war. The rest were extensively damaged or obliterated."

"What's this about Philadelphia being attacked?" Blade asked, goading the Russian.

Lysenko nodded. "They came in on ships. *Wooden* ships! Just like the ancient Vikings! There were thousands of them, and they were well armed. The design of their ships might have been antiquated, but their weapons were modern, at least the type prevalent before the war."

"There were thousands of ships?" Blade repeated doubtfully.

"No!" Lysenko said impatiently. "There were thousands of these Vikings. Our intelligence experts estimated there were no more than fifty ships in their fleet, with about one hundred Vikings for each ship. They came in under the cover of a heavy fog, and they were ashore before we knew it."

"Where were your ships?" Blade casually asked. "Weren't they patroling the port area?"

"Our ships?" Lysenko said, chuckling. "If you'd seen the condition of our navy, you wouldn't ask such a foolish question."

"In pitiful shape, huh?" Blade said.

"Worse than that," Lysenko disclosed. "Most of our ships were dry-docked decades ago. We lack the necessary repair facilities, and our manufacturing capability is practically nil. The few functional vessels we did have departed for the Motherland and then never returned. Several other vessels have ventured out to sea over the years, but they disappeared without a trace, just like your prisoners Geronimo told me about."

Geronimo began whistling a bit louder.

"Tell me about these Vikings," Blade urged.

"I only know what I saw detailed in the report," Lysenko said. "Approximately five thousand of them plundered and pillaged eastern Philadelphia for several hours, before our forces were mustered and pushed them back to the sea. They escaped in their ships, along with hundreds of captives and booty. Over six hundred of our men were killed, and seventy-four officers. I think the report said there were over fifteen hundred civilian casualties."

"Where did these Vikings come from?" Blade inquired.

"We don't know," Lysenko admitted. "We captured a dozen of them, and they're being held at a detention facility in Philadelphia while the Committee for State Security interrogates them."

"The Committee for State Security?"

"Yes. I believe the Committee was better known to America as the KGB," Lysenko stated.

"I recall reading about the KGB," Blade said.

"Yes," Lysenko commented proudly. "The KGB will elicit all the information we require on these Vikings, as they call themselves."

"And as far as you know," Blade stated, "the Vikings you captured are still alive?"

"So far as I know," Lysenko responded.

Blade pursed his lips.

"Do I get an AK-47?" Lysenko asked hopefully. He was mentally congratulating himself on his cleverness. It was true the information concerning the Vikings was classified, but he couldn't see where it was of any value to the Family or the Freedom Federation. They were hundreds of miles from any ocean. And should the Federation undertake to contact the Vikings, the outcome would be dubious. An alliance between the Vikings and the Freedom Federation was inconceivable. Essentially, he had just provided worthless information in exchange for a valuable weapon, a weapon he would need if he was to return to his unit. "Do I get an AK-47?" Lysenko repeated.

Blade nodded. "You were right. This information is important. You'll receive an AK-47 and all the ammo you can carry. Fair enough?"

Lysenko was beaming. "Fair enough."

"You must be hungry," Blade said. "Why don't you head toward B Block"—he pointed at the concrete structure—"and I'll be right behind you."

Lysenko nodded. "I can hardly wait to leave tomorrow." He took a step, then stopped. "It will be tomorrow, won't it?"

"It looks that way," Blade said.

Lysenko strode toward B Block.

Geronimo strolled over to Blade, and together they

slowly followed the Russian, staying about ten yards to his rear.

"He fell for it," Blade mentioned.

"So I noticed," Geronimo said, smirking.

"You overheard?" Blade asked.

"Every word," Geronimo confirmed.

"My compliments," Blade stated. "I expected him to willingly supply additional information, but I didn't expect the bit about the Vikings."

"I did exactly as you wanted," Geronimo commented. "You should have seen the look on his face when I told him about the alleged bloody shirt we found!" He laughed.

"There was no need to tell him we always allow anyone who leaves to take arms," Blade said. "He was right about that. No one would last two days out there without a weapon."

"You're going to inform Plato?" Geronimo inquired.

"Of course," Blade replied. "I want you to keep an eye on our Russian 'friend' while I go to Plato's cabin."

Geronimo stared into Blade's eyes. "You know what's going to happen, don't you?"

Blade sighed. "Yep. Plato will call a council of the Elders, and the Elders will decide to send the SEAL to Philadelphia."

"You don't have to go, you know," Geronimo said.

"Yes I do," Blade said disagreeing. "I'm the head Warrior. It's my responsibility. Besides, I've had the most experience driving the SEAL."

"Hickok can drive it," Geronimo remarked. "And I've practiced a few times."

"I appreciate the thought," Blade noted, thanking him, "but we both know Plato will want me to go."

"I get the impression you don't like these extended trips," Geronimo commented.

"I don't like being away from my family," Blade said sadly. "Jenny and little Gabe are my life. I don't get to see enough of them as it is. These long runs only make the situation worse."

"You could always relinquish your post and become

a Tiller," Geronimo suggested. "Or maybe a Weaver. You'd be real good with a needle."

Blade chuckled. "I'd belt you in the mouth, but I need you to watch Lysenko while I confer with Plato and the Elders."

"Will Hickok and I be going with you?" Geronimo asked.

"I don't know. Why?"

"Nathan isn't in the best frame of mind right now," Geronimo explained. "I had a talk with him today. He's pretty rattled over what happened to Sherry. He might be too distracted to perform effectively."

"Thanks for telling me," Blade said. "If that's the case, I'll have the Warriors draw lots. The two short straws will go, regardless of Triad affiliation."

"Like you did when you went to St. Louis," Geronimo commented.

"You've got it." Blade started to veer off toward the east.

"Hey!" Geronimo said.

"What?"

"Where do you think you'll be this time tomorrow?" Geronimo queried him.

Blade mused for a moment. "Probably the Twin Cities."

Geronimo grinned. "Your favorite vacation spot in all the world!"

5

As it turned out, Blade underestimated. The SEAL stopped for the night just south of what was once Mason City, Iowa. Like many cities and towns, Mason City had been abandoned during the war when the government had evacuated all citizens into the Rocky Mountain and Plains states. Now, Mason City was comprised of darkened ruins, situated in no-man's-land, with the Civilized Zone to the west, the Soviet-occupied territory to the southeast, and Chicago far to the east.

Blade had pushed the SEAL the first day. The SEAL had been the Founder's pride and joy. Kurt Carpenter had expended millions on the transport. Carpenter had foreseen the collapse of mass transportation and the public highway system. Accordingly, he'd provided for the Family's transportation needs by having a special vehicle constructed to his specifications. The scientists and engineers he'd employed were all experts in their chosen fields, and they'd given Carpenter his money's worth.

The SEAL was a prototype, revolutionary in its design and capabilities. The Solar Energized Amphibious or Land Recreational Vehicle—or SEAL, as it became known—was, as its name indicated, powered by the sun. The light was collected by a pair of solar panels affixed to the roof of the vanlike transport. The energy was converted and stored in unique batteries located in a lead-lined case under the SEAL. The floor was an impervious metal alloy. The body, the entire shell, was composed of a heat-resistant and virtually shatterproof plastic, fabricated to be indestructible. Four huge puncture-resistant tires, each four feet high and two feet wide, supported the vehicle.

Carpenter had wanted additional features added to the transport, and to incorporate them he'd turned to weapons specialists, to hired mercenaries. The military men had outfitted the vehicle with an array of armaments. Four toggle switches on the dashboard activated the SEAL's firepower. A pair of 50-caliber machine guns were hidden in recessed compartments under each front headlight. When the toggle marked M was thrown, a small metal plate would slide upward and the machine guns would automatically fire. A miniaturized surface-to-air missile was mounted in the roof above the driver's seat. Once the toggle labeled S was activated, a panel in the roof slid aside and a missile was launched. The missiles were heat-seeking Stingers with a range of ten miles. A rocket launcher was secreted in the center of the front grill, and the rocket was instantly fired if the R toggle was thrown. And finally, Carpenter had had the mercenaries include a flamethrower in the SEAL. It was an Army Surplus Model with an effective range of 20 feet. Located in the middle of the front fender, surrounded by layers of insulation, the flamethrower was activated when the F toggle was moved.

Blade gazed out the windshield at the night. The SEAL's body was tinted green, allowing those within to see out, but anyone outside was unable to view the interior. He stared up at the starry sky, then twisted in his bucket seat to check out his traveling companions. A console was situated between his bucket seat and the other bucket seat in the front of the transport. Behind the bucket seats, running the width of the vehicle, was another seat for passengers. The rear of the SEAL, comprising a third of its inside space, was devoted to a large storage area for spare parts, tools, and whatever provisions were necessary.

"We're makin' good time, ain't we, Big Guy?" Bertha asked. She was seated in the other bucket seat, her M-16 snuggled in her lap.

"So far, so good," Blade acknowledged. He glanced at the two passengers occupying the wide seat. "How are we holding up?"

Lieutenant Frol Lysenko was seated behind Bertha. His face conveyed his intense misery. Arms folded in front of him, hunched over dejectedly, he glared at the giant Warrior behind the wheel. "You lied to me!" he whined for the umpteenth time that day.

"No I didn't," Blade rejoined.

"Yes you did!" Lysenko snapped. "You promised me my freedom! You said I could have an AK-47 and ammo. Not to mention the canteen and jerky."

Blade smiled. "I beg to differ. I told you that you would be able to leave the Home, and you left it at sunrise this morning. There are several canteens and five pounds of venison jerky stored in the back of the SEAL. Take your pick."

Lysenko glowered at the Warrior.

"As for the AK-47," Blade went on, "we gave you one, remember? It's not our fault you didn't want it."

"Damn you!" Lysenko spat. "What good would it have done me? Sure, you offered me an AK-47 this morning! And you also offered me ten magazines of ammo . . . but it wasn't AK-47 ammo!"

Blade shrugged. "I kept my word. I promised to give you an AK-47 and all the ammunition you could carry. I never said the ammo would be for the AK-47."

"You devious son of a bitch!" Lysenko said.

Bertha glanced at Blade. "Do you want me to bop this sucker for you?"

"No need," Blade replied.

"I wouldn't let him talk to me that way," Bertha commented.

Lysenko made the mistake of leaning forward, sneering. "Oh? And what would you do, woman?" He accented the last word contemptuously.

The M-16 was up and around in the blink of the eye, the barrel rammed into Lysenko's nose.

The Russian gulped and blinked.

Bertha smiled sweetly, her brown eyes dancing with mirth. "You ever talk to me like that again, honky, and I'll waste you on the spot. Got that, ugly?"

Lysenko nodded.

Blade grinned. He enjoyed Bertha's company immensely. They had shared many an adventure over the years, ever since Alpha Triad had rescued her from the Watchers in Thief River Falls. She had assisted them in the Twin Cities, and later had been of inestimable help in the Family's fight against the wicked Doktor. Although she had been born and reared in the Twin Cities, and spent most of her life involved in the bitter gang warfare there, Bertha had been accepted as a Warrior based on her prior service to the Family. Blade, Hickok, and Geronimo had appealed to the Elders to approve her nomination. Hickok had made a rare, yet oddly eloquent speech calling for her installation as a Warrior, saying at one point, as Blade recalled: "If Bertha ain't fit to be a Warrior, then neither am I, or Blade, or Geronimo, or Rikki. Bertha may not have been raised in the Home, but she's as Family as can be. And, more importantly, she's a born Warrior in her heart. That feisty female can whip her weight in wildcats. So you'd best approve her application, or she'll most likely storm in here and punch you out." Blade could still remember the amused expressions of the assembled Elders.

Bertha turned toward the fourth member of their little group. He was seated behind Blade, dressed in a fancy gray shirt and trousers, both tailor-made for him by the Family Weavers. The shirt had wide lapels and black buttons; the pants legs were flared at the bottom. He wore a wide black belt with a silver buckle. Nestled in a black shoulder holster under each arm was an L.A.R. Grizzly. The Grizzly was an automatic pistol with a seven-shot magazine, chambered for the devastating .45 Winchester Magnum cartridge. Its grips were black, but the rest of it was shining silver. The man wore his black hair neatly trimmed around the ears, and a full black mustache added to his strikingly handsome appearance. "What's with you, Sundance?" Bertha asked. "You've hardly said a word this whole trip so far."

The Warrior called Sundance shrugged. "What did you want me to say?"

"Anything would've been nice," Bertha remarked. "You sure ain't the talkative type, are you?"

"Guess not," Sundance responded in his low voice.

Bertha pointed at the Grizzlies. "I've been meanin' to ask you. Are you any good with those pistols of yours?"

"Fair," Sundance laconically answered.

"You as good as Hickok?" Bertha inquired.

"Maybe," Sundance said.

Bertha threw back her head and laughed. She reached over and tapped Blade on the shoulder. "Did you hear this idiot? He thinks he's as good as White Meat!" White Meat was her pet term for Hickok.

"I've seen Sundance practice," Blade mentioned. "He's real fast, Bertha."

"Maybe so," Bertha stated, "but there ain't no way he could beat White Meat, and you know it."

"That depends," Blade said.

"On what?" Bertha retorted.

"On how you mean it," Blade explained. "If you mean fast on the draw, then I'd have to agree with you. I've never seen anyone who can draw as fast as Hickok. But, on the other hand, if you mean fast in firing a gun, then Sundance might have the edge."

"What?" Bertha said skeptically.

Blade nodded toward Sundance. "He uses automatic pistols, Bertha, Hickok prefers his Colt Pythons, and they're revolvers."

"So?" Bertha responded.

"So have you ever compared a pistol and a revolver?" Blade asked.

"No," Bertha admitted.

"You should sometime," Blade recommended. "We have a lot of books in the Family library on guns. Dozens and dozens of books, covering everything from bullet-making to replacing busted stocks. We know pistols and revolvers were popular before the Big Blast, and we also know there was considerable controversy over whether a pistol or a revolver could fire faster."

"What do you think?" Bertha queried.

"I'm getting to that," Blade said. "The experts debated the pros and cons of both types. Automatic pistols, as a rule, hold more rounds than a standard revolver. Sundance's Grizzlies, for instance, hold seven rounds in the magazine, while Hickok's Pythons usually hold five."

"Five?" Bertha said, surprised. "But the cylinders in the Pythons can hold six bullets."

"True," Blade conceded, "but Hickok seldom keeps a round under the hammer. Most professionals don't. Less chance of an accident that way." He paused. "The revolver is normally thicker and slightly bulkier than a pistol. But in reliability, when it comes to things like jamming and dud rounds, the revolver is considered superior. In the accuracy department, both are even when used by a skilled gunman. Revolvers can handle broader load ranges than most pistols, and that's a plus."

"But what about bein' fast?" Bertha interrupted

impatiently.

"I'm getting to that," Blade reiterated. "When it comes to speed, you have to keep in mind the type of revolver we're talking about. With a single-action revolver, you have to pull back the hammer before squeezing the trigger, and that definitely slows you down. Hickok's Pythons, on the other hand, are double-action, meaning he can fire either way, by squeezing just the trigger or by pulling back the hammer and then shooting. Double-actions have an edge over single-actions in that respect."

"But what about bein' fast?" Bertha asked, sounding peeved.

"I'm getting to that," Blade repeated again.

"This year or next?" Bertha rejoined.

Blade grinned. "In our last trade exchange with the Civilized Zone, we received two stopwatches."

"Two what?" Bertha inquired.

"Stopwatches," Blade said. "You know what a watch is, don't you?"

"Of course!" Bertha stated. "Do you think I'm a dummy? I saw a lot of watches on the Watchers . . ." She stopped, then laughed. "Watches on the Watchers! Get it?"

Blade sighed. "I get it."

"I know the Family didn't use watches years ago," Bertha mentioned. "But I've seen a few around since you started tradin' with the rest of the Freedom Federation. So what's a stopwatch?"

"It can measure how fast someone moves," Blade detailed.

"Really?"

"Really," Blade affirmed. "And Geronimo used one to time Hickok, to see how fast Nathan could draw and fire five shots."

"How did White Meat do?" Bertha asked him.

"Hickok drew and fired all five shots in his right Python in two-fifths of a second," Blade answered.

"Is that fast?" Bertha asked.

"Let me put it to you this way," Blade said. "If you'd blinked, you would have missed it."

"That fast, huh?" Sundance interjected.

"Yep," Blade confirmed.

Bertha smiled triumphantly. "So that means White Meat would beat Sundance's cute butt no problem, right?"

"Not necessarily," Blade said.

"Cute butt?" Sundance interjected again.

"Now what the hell does that mean?" Bertha demanded of Blade.

"Cute butt?" Sundance repeated.

"It means," Blade said, "Hickok can draw his Pythons faster than Sundance can draw his Grizzlies . . . ."

Bertha stuck her tongue out at Sundance.

" . . . but I don't think Hickok can empty his guns faster than Sundance can empty his," Blade concluded.

"What?" Bertha stated. "But you just said—"

"I wish you would listen to me," Blade said, cutting her short. "Yes, Hickok is faster on the draw, but only by a fraction. And yes, his double-action revolvers are the equal of most pistols. But I've seen both men shoot, and I believe Sundance can empty his Grizzlies a teensy bit faster. Does that answer your question?"

"It doesn't answer mine!" Lieutenant Lysenko snapped.

Blade turned in his seat. "You have a question?"

"Yes!" Lysenko snapped. "When the hell are you going to turn off the overhead light and let me sleep in peace and quiet? All this babble is extremely annoying!"

Bertha looked at Blade. "*Please* let me bop him in the head!"

"We need him," Blade told her.

"Need me?" Lysenko said. "For what? You won't get any more information out of me, not after the way you tricked me. I don't see why you brought me along!"

"Consider yourself our tour guide," Blade commented.

"You made the biggest mistake of your life when you screwed me over," Lysenko warned.

"Oh!" Bertha exclaimed. "Somebody catch me! I

think I'm goin' to faint from fright!" She tittered.

"Have your fun while you can," Lysenko said. "What goes around, comes around."

"Blade," Sundance said.

"Yeah?"

"Can anyone see inside when the overhead light is on?" Sundance inquired, staring out his side of the SEAL.

"No. No one can see inside, no matter what. Why?" Blade replied.

Sundance motioned with his head. "Because we have company."

Blade stared into the night. "Where?"

"At the edge of trees. Keep your eyes peeled," Sundance said. "You'll see them moving from trunk to trunk."

Although he knew they were invisible inside the transport, Blade reached up and switched off the overhead light anyway. If they had to open the doors, the light would reveal them to any foes outside. He scanned the row of trees on his side of the transport. The SEAL was parked on the shoulder of U.S. Highway 65 two miles south of Mason City. Like the majority of highways and roads, U.S. Highway 65 was in deplorable, but passable, shape. Potholes dotted the highway, intermixed with ruts, buckled sections, and even stretches where the road had been totally destroyed by the twin ravages of time and nature. The SEAL, with its colossal tires, impervious body, and amphibious mode, could circumvent virtually any obstacle. And knowing the SEAL was bulletproof and fire-resistant, Blade hadn't hesitated to park the transport in the open, on the side of the highway. They hadn't seen a single soul, not one other vehicle, the whole day. The likelihood of being ambushed was extremely remote. Or so Blade had thought.

"I see them!" Bertha exclaimed. "Lordy! There's a lot of them!"

Blade could see them too. Dark shadows flitting from cover to cover, slowly advancing toward the transport, illuminated by the half-moon in the eastern sky.

"What do we do?" Bertha asked.

Blade deliberated. They could stay put and trust to the SEAL to protect them from harm. But what if one of those shadows was armed with a hand grenade? What if the grenade was tossed under the SEAL, where the transport was most vulnerable? Or what if they had a bazooka? Blade considered simply driving off, but the act of starting the engine might precipitate an assault. The SEAL's firepower was nullified by the angle the shadows were using to approach; the machine guns, the rocket launcher, and the flamethrower were all aimed to the front of the vehicle, while the shadows were coming up on the driver's side. He had to make a decision, and he had to do it quickly. "We need a diversion, something to draw their attention while I start the SEAL."

"Leave it to me," Sundance said, and he was in motion even as he spoke, flinging the door open and diving to the ground.

The shadows detected the movement of the door, and a fusillade of gunfire erupted from the trees, handgun and rifle fire, the slugs striking the SEAL, many of them whining as they ricocheted.

Sundance rolled on his shoulders as he struck the earth, and he came up with a Grizzly in each hand as the shadows charged from the forest. The Grizzlies thundered, one shot after another, eight shots in swift succession, and with every shot a shadow dropped, some screeching in agony as they fell.

Blade clutched at the ignition and twisted the key, and as the engine turned over there was a peculiar smacking sound from behind him and something wet sprayed onto his right arm and the back of his neck. He glanced over his shoulder.

Lieutenant Frol Lysenko was dead. Two of the wild shots fired by the onrushing shadows had narrowly missed Sundance and entered the open door. Lysenko had been struck in the forehead and the chin. The top slug had blown out the back of his head, splattering hair, brains, and blood over the seats. The chin shot had shattered his mouth; part of his tongue and four teeth hung by a thread of flesh from the ruined hole of his mouth.

"Sundance!" Blade bellowed. "Now!"

Sundance fired once more, downing a screaming shadow, and then he spun and vaulted into the SEAL, through the flapping door, as Blade accelerated, flooring the pedal, and the SEAL lurched ahead. Sundance landed on the floor, crouched over, his right elbow on the seat in a pool of Lysenko's blood. He twisted and slammed the door shot.

The shadows peppered the transport with gunfire as it sped off.

Bertha stared over the pile of supplies, out the rear of the SEAL. "We're leavin' them turkeys in the dust!" she exclaimed.

"We'll go another twenty miles, then stop for the night," Blade said, abruptly noticing he'd failed to turn on the headlights, an oversight he immediately remedied. He looked over his right shoulder at the Russian. "Damn!"

"What's the big deal?" Bertha asked. "It couldn't have happened to a nicer asshole!"

"We needed him," Blade stated.

"We can get by without that dork," Bertha said.

Sundance rose to a sitting position in the seat.

They drove in silence for several minutes.

Blade flicked on the overhead light and glanced in the rearview mirror at the dead officer. "Damn!" he fumed again. He slammed on the brakes and the transport slewed to a top. "Get him out of here!"

Sundance reached across Lysenko's body and unlatched the far door. He eased the door open, placed his right brown leather boot on Lysenko's chest, and kicked.

The mortal remains of Lieutenant Frol Lysenko pitched head-first into the night.

6

Four days later.

"What's the name of the town ahead?" Blade asked.

Bertha consulted the map in her lap. "It's some dinky place called Huntsburg." She checked the population index on the reverse side of the map. "The map doesn't say how many people lived there before the Big Blast."

They were in Ohio. The SEAL was idling on top of a low rise. A cluster of buildings was visible about a quarter of a mile ahead on U.S. Highway 322.

"How am I doing?" Bertha queried Blade. "Am I readin' this sucker okay?"

"You're doing just fine," Blade complimented her.

Bertha grinned. "Lordy! It sure is fine knowin' how to read!"

"You've come a long way," Blade said. "I know how hard you've applied yourself over the past year or so, taking all of those classes. It must have been very difficult."

"It wasn't easy," Bertha acknowledged. "But the Elders are good teachers."

The Elders were responsible for the Family's educational regimen. They taught classes on the basics, on history, geography, math, reading, writing, and more, to the family children. The Elders also offered advanced courses based on their individual expertise. The Home was unique in this respect. For most of America, public education, like all other cultural institutions, was nonexistent.

Bertha ran her left hand over the map, delighted at her progress. When she'd first arrived at the Home, she'd been illiterate. Now, thanks to the Family, she could read and write quite well. She took particular delight in signing her name, and had developed a flamboyant flourish as a token of her pride.

"Huntsburg doesn't appear to be big enough to pose any problems," Blade mentioned. "But stay sharp! We can't take any chances! We learned that the other night." He glanced in the rearview mirror at Sundance. "I know this is your first run away from the Home. You did real well against those goons, but you still don't have any idea how rough it gets out here. You never know when something will pop out at you. So keep your eyes open."

"You don't have to tell me twice," Sundance said.

Blade slowly drove toward Huntsburg. The four days since the last incident had been relatively uneventful. As on all his previous trips, Blade had deliberately avoided cities and large towns. Even smaller settlements, when there was any indication of habitation, were skirted. From prior harsh experience, Blade had learned the futility of foolishly relying on receiving a friendly reception *anywhere.* There were too many savage bands, too many scavengers, raiders, and worse roaming the landscape to permit the needless taking of any risks. Blade prevented trouble by avoiding it. The SEAL was capable of navigating any terrain, so bypassing cities and towns by swinging a loop through the contryside was an easy task. If the town or hamlet was a small one, lacking any evidence of being inhabited, Blade would gamble and drive straight through to save time. Usually, his instincts in this regard were reliable.

But not this time.

A small business section appeared ahead. A dilapidated restaurant was on the right, a crumbling bar on the left. Ancient signs, too faint to read, adorned some of the other ramshackle structures.

"Looks like nobody's home," Bertha remarked.

Blade scanned the cracked sidewalks and the shattered windows. Huntsburg seemed to be a ghost town.

"Think we can stop and stretch our legs?" Bertha asked. "It's almost noon, and we've been drivin' since dawn."

"I don't see why not," Blade replied. He angled the SEAL up to the curb in front of the restaurant. "It looks like the looters tore this town apart during the war," he noted.

"Sure is a dump now," Bertha agreed, leaning out her open window.

Blade braked, then shut off the engine.

Bertha opened her door and dropped to the sidewalk, her M-16 in her hands. "I'm gonna take a look around."

"Just be careful," Blade advised her.

"If you don't mind," Sundance spoke up, "I'd like to go with Bertha. My legs are getting cramped from all this sitting."

"Go ahead," Blade said. "I'll stick with the SEAL."

Sundance climbed out his side of the transport, closed the door, and joined Bertha.

Bertha cocked her head, scrutinizing him. "Why'd you want to come with me?"

"Do I need a reason?" Sundance inquired.

"Just so you ain't got the hots for my body," Bertha said. "It's already spoken for."

"So I heard," Sundance stated.

Bertha's jaw muscles tightened. "What's that crack supposed to mean?"

Sundance started walking along the pitted sidewalk, bearing to the east. "It means I don't have the hots for your body."

Bertha quickly caught up with him. "You don't?" she asked, sounding surprised.

"Nope," Sundance told her.

Bertha looked down at herself. "Why not? What's wrong with my body?"

"Nothing," Sundance said, surveying the street ahead. "It's one of the nicest bodies I've seen."

Bertha beamed. "It is? Really ?"

Sundance glanced at her. "I don't lie."

They strolled in the sunshine for several moments.

"What do you mean by nice?" Bertha asked.

Sundance suddenly stopped. "Did you hear something?"

"No." Bertha studied the nearby buildings. "Why?"

"I don't know . . ." Sundance said, and resumed walking.

"Mind if I ask you a question?" Bertha mentioned.

"No."

"Why'd you pick the name Sundance? I know White Meat took the handle Hickok 'cause he's wacko about Wild Bill Hickok. What about you?" Bertha probed. "Was there some old-time gunfighter named Sundance?"

"There was," Sundance replied.

"Ahhh!"

"But he wasn't exactly a gunfighter," Sundance explained. "His real name was Harry Longabaugh, and he was an outlaw in the Old West. I read about him in a book called the *Encyclopedia of Western Gunfighters.* He was nowhere near as famous as Wild Bill Hickok, and far less deadly."

"Then why'd you pick his name?" Bertha asked.

Sundance grinned and looked at her. "Because I like it. The name has a certain ring to it."

"Sure does," Bertha agreed. Sundance cocked his head, listening.

Bertha glanced over her left shoulder. They were a block from the transport. "Maybe we shouldn't stray too far from the SEAL," she suggested.

Sundance stopped. "Fine by me." He gazed up at a broken second-floor window across the highway. "There it is again."

"There what is?" Bertha queried.

"Didn't you hear it?" Sundance asked.

"Hear what?"

"A sort of low whistle," Sundance said, moving to the edge of the sidewalk. "I've heard it several times already."

"It must be the wind," Bertha speculated.

Sundance held up his right hand. "But there's no breeze," he pointed out.

That was when Bertha heard it too: a low, warbling whistle coming from the empty office to their right. She peered into the inky gloom of the interior, trying to perceive movement. What could it be? she asked herself. A bird of some kind? A small animal?

But it was neither.

Bertha was just beginning to turn, to head back to the

SEAL, when she discerned a bulky shape materializing out of the darkness shrouding the office building. A stray shaft of sunlight glinted off a metallic object. "Sundance!" she shouted in alarm, not waiting to determine if the figure was friend or foe. The M-16 snapped up, and she fired from the waist, on automatic, her rounds chipping away the jagged pieces of glass remaining in the front window of the office and striking the shape inside, propelling it from sight.

Someone screamed in agony.

And all hell broke loose.

Over a dozen attackers burst from the buildings lining U.S. Highway 322, charging through doorways and bounding over windowsills, some with guns blazing, others armed with knives, swords, hatchets, and whatever else they could get their hands on. All of them were bestial in aspect, with unkempt, bedraggled hair and apparel. Most wore tattered clothing or filthy animal hides and skins. They jabbered and yelled as they surged from hiding.

Sundance was in motion even as the first scavenger rushed from a doorway across the highway. His hands flashed up and out, leveling the Grizzlies, and his first shot boomed while the scavenger was raising a rifle, the impact of the .45 Winchester Magnum slug lifting the scavenger from his feet and slamming him against the wall. Sundance swiveled as a filthy raven-haired woman appeared on a balcony on the other side of 322, a crossbow in her hands. She was aiming at Bertha when both Grizzlies thundered, and the top of her head imitated the erupting of a volcano. The female scavenger dropped the crossbow, tottered, and fell, crashing into the balcony railing and through the railing as the rotted wood splintered and gave way. Sundance never saw her fall. He had already spun to the left, finding a trio of scavengers sprinting toward them, spilling from the mouth of the alley, blocking their retreat to the SEAL. One of the scavengers was armed with a spear, and his hand was sweeping back for the throw when Sundance shot him in the right eye, jerking his head to the right, and sending the scavenger tumbling to the sidewalk.

Bertha was firing her M-16 as rapidly as targets presented themselves. "We've got to get the hell out of here!" she shouted.

"To the SEAL!" Sundance replied, squeezing both triggers, both Grizzlies bucking in his hands, and the two scavengers between the SEAL and them went down in a jumbled mass of flaying arms and legs.

Bertha took off, blasting a tall scavenger shooting at them with a revolver from the roof of the bar. His head whipped back and he vanished from view.

Sundance followed Bertha, covering her, killing two more scavengers sprinting across the street. Bullets smacked into the wall behind them. Something tugged at his left sleeve. They were still three-quarters of a block distant from the SEAL when he heard the loud pounding to his rear. He whirled.

A mob of maddened, bloodthirsty scavengers was pounding toward them, bellowing their rage and brandishing their assorted weapons. A grungy character in the lead was sighting a Winchester.

Sundance fired both Grizzlies, and the grungy scavenger was hurled from his feet to collide with another scavenger coming up behind him.

Bertha shot a scavenger on the other side of the street.

"Bertha!" Sundance yelled as an arrow streaked past his right cheek.

Bertha glanced over her right shoulder, spying the maddened throng pursuing them. "Shit!" she exploded, turning to support Sundance.

Sundance risked a look toward the SEAL, and he was surprised to see the transport roaring from the curb and racing down the center of the highway. The front end suddenly swerved toward the sidewalk, and Sundance leaped, his left arm catching Bertha around the waist. "What the hell!" she blurted, even as his momentum carried both of them over the lower sill of a demolished window and onto the hard wood floor of a deserted building.

Outside, the 50-caliber machine guns opened up, almost drowning out the shrieks of the decimated scavengers. The chatter of the machine guns was followed by a tremendous explosion. Screams and wails punctuated the din. And then there was a sibilant hissing, and smoke wafted from the nearby structures.

Sundance and Bertha slowly rose, coughing, their nostrils tingling with an acrid odor.

Sundance stepped over the windowsill, the Grizzlies leveled, prepared for more combat.

But there wouldn't be any.

Bodies seemed to be everywhere. Scorched, blasted, bloody bodies and body parts littered the highway and the sidewalks. Gray smoke hovered overhead. Whimpers and cries rose on the air.

The SEAL was idling in the middle of the street, not ten feet away. Tendrils of smoke rose from the front fender and the grill.

Sundance saw a scavenger with shredded stumps below the waist flopping on the ground and whining. Near the front end of the SEAL was a blackened, smoking pair of boots, minus their owner. On the sidewalk to the right was a severed right arm, the fingers still twitching. The tableau was grisly, ghastly beyond belief. Sundance felt sick to his stomach and grimaced.

Bertha grinned. "When it comes to wastin' chumps, Blade is almost as good as White Meat." She had seen the Seal in action before, and knew firsthand the havoc it could wreak.

Sundance stared at the twitching fingers, simultaneously fascinated and repulsed.

Bertha looked at the Warrior in gray, startled by the loathing reflection in his expression. "Ain't you ever seen the SEAL kick butt before?" she asked.

Sundance shook his head.

"You must of seen worse than this," Bertha stated. "How about when the Home was attacked while Blade was off in Denver? I was told the Home was knee-deep in bodies."

"I wasn't a Warrior then," Sundance replied absently. "I took a hit early on in the siege and missed most of the action. They had the mess cleaned up by the time I was released from the infirmary."

"Well, don't let it get to you," Bertha advised. "It

was them or us."

A door slammed, and Blade came around the front of the SEAL, a Commando Arms Carbine in his hands. "Are you two all right?" he inquired. His eyes alighted on Sundance. "Sundance?"

Sundance grimly nodded. "I'm fine." The right corner of his mouth twisted upward. "If I can't take this, I don't deserve to be a Warrior."

"We've got to get out of here," Blade said. "We don't know who might come to investigate all the firing."

Bertha nudged Sundance. "Let's go! Get your cute rump in the SEAL."

Sundance glanced at her in disapproval. "I wish you would stop that."

"Stop what?"

"Stop talking about my . . . rump," Sundance said, walking toward the transport.

"I'm just returning the favor," Bertha said.

"What favor?" Sundance asked as he opened the door.

"You said I had a nice body. Can I help it if I feel the same way about your buns?" Bertha stated.

Blade grinned and ran to the driver's door. He clambered into the SEAL and deposited his Commando on the console.

Sundance and Bertha took their seats.

"Here we go," Blade said, gunning the motor, weaving between the corpses as he bore to the east. "If all goes well, we should reach Philadelphia in two days at the most. Possibly sooner. It all depends on what we run into along the way. I've managed to keep well north of the Soviet lines, but we could still run into one of their patrols. Even the Technics."

"Aren't the Technics those bozos in Chicago?" Bertha queried. "The ones who forced you to drive the SEAL to New York City?"

"They're the ones," Blade confirmed. "I imagine the Family hasn't heard the last of them."

They drove past the rusted wreckage of a bus.

"You were right about one thing, Blade," Sundance

commented, in the process of reloading the clips in his Grizzlies.

"What was that?" Blade asked.

"You never know when something or someone will pop out at you," Sundance stated. "You have no warning whatsoever." He paused. "I think the next time I take a leak, I'll do it with a gun in one hand."

7

The SEAL wheeled off the road, its huge tires pulverizing all the weeds, bushes, small trees, and every other minor obstruction in its path. The transport cut across a field and into a dense forest.

Blade, carefully negotiating a path between the larger trees, glanced at Bertha. "We did it!" he said, elated.

"We've been lucky," Bertha declared.

"Either that, or there aren't as many Russians in this area as we were led to believe," Sundance chimed in.

The afternoon sun was in the western sky. White clouds floated on the air. A rabbit, startled by the mechanical behemoth plowing through the woods, hopped off in fright.

"If this map is right," Bertha said, hunched over the map in her lap, "then we're in what was once called Valley Forge National Historical Park."

"This was a park?" Blade queried, braking under an immense maple tree.

"That's what the map says," Bertha insisted.

Blade turned the engine off. He thought of their good fortune since the firefight in Huntsburg. Two days of travel, two days of sticking to the secondary roads and bypassing every town, no matter how small, and they were now close to their goal, to Philadelphia. Twice they'd spotted helicopters in the distance. In both cases, the copters were flying on the southern horizon. Both times, Blade had pulled the transport into nearby trees until the helicopter disappeared.

"So what's the plan?" Sundance inquired.

"We hide here until dark, then start walking," Blade answered.

"We're leavin' the SEAL here?" Bertha queried.

"We don't have any choice," Blade said. "Even at night, the SEAL would stand out as being completely different from anything the Reds have. We'll leave it here and commandeer a jeep or truck or a civilian vehicle if necessary."

"Why didn't we run into any roadblocks in the last hundred miles or so?" Sundance asked. "We know the Soviets control southern Pennsylvania. Why didn't we bring that radio along to monitor them?"

"It's too valuable to the Family to risk our losing it," Blade said. "As for any roadblocks, they'd be on the highways, and we've stuck to the less-traveled roads. Maybe, as you said, there aren't many troops in this area. Maybe they're concentrated in Philadelphia. Or maybe they don't use roadblocks anymore. Remember, it's been a century since the war. This area has been under their thumb for a hundred years. Resistance probably died out long ago. They haven't been attacked here in decades. Maybe security is lax because they don't have any need for it."

"I hope you're right, Big Guy," Bertha said. "It'll make our job a little easier."

"How will we find where these Vikings are being held?" Sundance questioned.

"We'll find a way," Blade stated.

Bertha snickered. "I love a person with confidence!"

Which explained her affection for Hickok, Blade mentally noted as he turned in his bucket seat. "Sundance, look in the rear section, in the right-hand corner."

Sundance shifted and began climbing over the top of his seat. "What am I looking for?"

"Find a green blanket," Blade directed. "It's folded in half."

Sundance, on his hands and knees, gingerly moved over their mound of supplies. "I see it," he said.

"Lift up the green blanket," Blade directed. "What do you see?"

Sundance raised the folded blanket. "I see uniforms." He leaned closer. "Russian uniforms."

"Bring them here," Blade ordered. "There should be one for each of us."

"Russian uniforms?" Bertha said. "Did the Weavers make them?"

"We took them from the bodies of the four soldiers killed near the Home," Blade detailed. "The Weavers did a rush job on them the night before we left. Washed them. Patched up the bullet holes and tears. The hard part was constructing a serviceable uniform for me. All of them were way too small. The Weavers had to sew two of the uniforms together, and they did a dandy job."

Sundance clambered into the middle seat, the uniforms under his left arm. "Here." He handed one to Bertha. "And this looks like the big one," he said, extending the uniform toward Blade.

"Thanks." Blade took the uniform. "This is it. We'll change into these."

"Now?" Bertha asked.

"Just so you get it done before dark," Blade replied. "Why?"

"I don't know," Bertha said uncertainly. "I think I'll change outside."

"Whatever you want," Blade commented. "Or we can change outside and you can stay here."

"No. No need." Bertha opened her door, put the Russian uniform under her left arm, and grabbed the M-16 in her right hand. "I'll be back in a sec." She slid to the grass, then closed the door behind her.

A squirrel stared at her from the top of a nearby tree.

Frowning, Bertha moved away from the transport. What the hell was wrong with her? Since when did she become bashful about her naked body? She'd never cared one way or the other before. Before joining the Family.

The squirrel started chattering.

Bertha walked around a large trunk. Off to her left

was a thicket. She slowly stepped toward it, musing. The Family had changed her, that was for sure. And she didn't know if she liked all the changes. Being able to read was terrific, the thrill of her life. But what about the rest of the changes? What about being more subdued, about being less prone to speak her mind when something or someone bugged her? What about being embarrassed to change her clothes in front of two men? Two friends!

Or were they?

Blade was a friend. There was no doubt about that. One of the best she had. But what about Sundance? She hardly knew the man well enough to call him a friend. And if he wasn't a friend, then what was he? A fellow Warrior, of course. But beyond that? She had to admit to herself she was attracted to Sundance, and the disclosure bothered her. A lot. She had intentionally avoided becoming involved with anyone for ages. After what had happened with Hickok, who could blame her? she asked herself. She had given her heart to the blond gunman, and he had inadvertently hurt her to the depths of her soul. Her heart had been crushed. She'd never let on, never let Hickok or anyone else know how torn apart she felt. Surprisingly, the ache hadn't diminished with the passage of time. Every time she saw Hickok and Sherry together, she wanted to run off somewhere and cry. The "old" Bertha would have punched Sherry's lights out and forced herself upon the gunfighter.

What had happened to her?

Was it really the influence exerted by the Family? Or was the cause some quality inside of her? Had she matured? Was that it? She remembered Plato saying once that a person had to mature to grow. Was she becoming wiser, or dumber? What woman in her right mind would allow the man of her dreams to slip through her fingers?

Bertha sadly shook her head.

There were so many questions, and never enough answers.

Bertha stopped, concealed from the transport by the

dense thicket. She dropped the uniform onto the ground, then leaned the M-16 on a low branch. Preoccupied with her reflection, she removed her green fatigue shirt and her belt.

The underbrush to her rear rustled.

Bertha scooped up the M-16 and twirled, her alert eyes scanning the vegetation.

Nothing.

Her nerves must be on edge, she decided, and lowered the M-16 to the ground. It served her right for acting like a damp wimp, for leaving the SEAL to change her clothes. She stooped and picked up the shirt to the Russian uniform.

Footsteps pounded on the earth behind her.

Bertha released the uniform shirt and bent over, grabbing at the M-16. Before she could grip it, arms encircled her waist and drove her to her knees. She instinctively rammed her left elbow back and up, and was gratified when she connected and someone grunted. The arms encircling her slackened slightly, and she repeated the move with her right arm. At the same time, she butted her head backwards.

Both blows landed.

There was a gasp, and the arms holding her slipped away.

Bertha lunged for the M-16, sweeping it into her hands and rolling to her feet, her fingers on the trigger. She glimpsed her assailant and froze. "Son of a bitch!" she exclaimed.

It was a kid!

Her attacker was a boy of 12 or 13, a pudgy youth dressed in tattered rags. He was on his hands and knees, blood trickling from his nose, peering up at her in abject fear.

Bertha started to lower the M-16.

The boy bolted. He was up and gone like a panicked colt, racing back the way he came, heading into the brush.

"Wait!" Bertha called.

The youth ignored her. He darted between two trees and disappeared.

"Damn!" Bertha muttered, starting after him. She took three steps, then realized she was naked from the waist up. "Doubledamn!" She turned, spied her fatigue shirt, and snatched it from the grass. What the hell was a kid doing out here in the middle of nowhere? She jogged after him, donning her shirt as she ran, reaching the two trees and pausing to button her front.

Where was he?

Bertha studied the ground, wishing she could read tracks like Geronimo. A twig snapped, and she looked up in time to see the boy duck around a boulder ten yards in front of her.

There was no way she was going to let him escape!

Bertha took off, sprinting to the boulder and around it, but the boy was gone.

Now where?

The youth came into view 20 yards to the right, visible as he passed a tree and scurried into a patch of high weeds.

Bertha ran to the weeds and stopped, surveying the terrain. The weed patch was 15 yards in diameter, and the weeds were 3 to 5 feet in height. A hill rose on the other side of the weeds, its slope covered with trees and brush.

The boy appeared about ten yards up the hill. He glanced over his left shoulder at Bertha, then kept going.

The sucker sure could run! Bertha hurried after him, crossing the weeds and reaching the base of the hill. Close up, the hill was a lot steeper than it had seemed. She hurried up the slope, her powerful legs churning.

The fleeing boy became visible again, this time near the crest of the hill. He stopped, watching her ascend.

"Wait!" Bertha yelled.

To her surprise, the boy grinned.

"I won't hurt you!" Bertha shouted. "I just want to talk to you!"

The boy flipped her the finger.

"Wait there!" Bertha cried.

Instead, the boy turned and continued over the crest

of the hill.

Smart-ass kid!

Bertha chugged up the slope, halting when she reached the top. The other side of the hill was an eerie landscape. A fire, probably caused by a lightning strike, had fried the vegetation to a cinder. Dozens of blackened, charred trunks dotted the hillside.

The boy was almost to the bottom. He stopped, gazed up at her, and laughed.

What the hell did he think this was? A game? Bertha pounded down the slope after him. Below the hill was a field, and she saw the boy reach it and accelerate. For a pudgy kid, he sure could move! Her black boots crunched on the brittle burnt grass as she raced to the bottom of the hill. A sudden pain in her left side caused her to check her pursuit. She doubled over, breathing heavily.

Pudgy was nearly to the far side of the field.

Bertha inhaled deeply, trying to alleviate the discomfort. How far was she from the SEAL? she wondered. Too far. She couldn't keep following this kid, not when Blade and Sundance might become worried and come looking for her. If the brat didn't want to talk to her, that was his business. She was on a mission.

Besides, her chest ached like crazy!

Bertha slowly straightened.

The boy was on the other side of the field, simply standing there, his hands on his hips, watching her.

Bertha flipped him the finger.

The boy's mouth dropped.

Bertha turned, grinning. That ought to teach the little snot! She began retracing her path up the hill.

There was a loud scream from across the field.

Bertha spun.

The boy was gone.

Bertha frowned as she moved to the edge of the field. For some reason, the fire had not scorched the weeds and brush below the hill. She squinted, trying to see the trees on the far side clearly.

There was no hint of what had happened to the boy.

Bertha hesitated. She should get back to the SEAL, return to Blade and report. But what if the kid was really in trouble? She couldn't just leave. If the brat was trying to fake her out, she'd give him a lesson he'd never forget.

Like a bust in the chops.

Bertha jogged toward the woods, constantly scanning for movement. The farther she went, the more concerned she became about the boy. The forest was too dangerous, what with all the wild animals and the mutants, for a young boy. His threads had been pitiful. He must be on his own, wresting an existence from the land as best he could.

A shadowy shape materialized in the forest ahead.

Bertha halted, raising the M-16. Whatever it was, the thing was enormous. She waited for it to move. And waited.

What the hell was it?

Bertha cautiously advanced. She suddenly realized the shape wasn't that of a monstrous creature.

It was a log cabin!

The cabin was situated approximately 30 yards into the trees. The surrounding forest served to render it invisible except at close range. Two windows, both with their glass panes intact, fronted the field. Between the windows was a door.

An open door.

Bertha tensed, suspecting a trap. Maybe the boy had deliberately led her here. She stepped toward the cabin, determined to get to the bottom of this. Her boots eased forward, step by step.

The cabin seemed to be uninhabited.

Bertha reached a cleared space, a strip about ten yards wide, forming a semicircle in front of the door. She advanced toward the cabin, proceeding cautiously. Her M-16 at the ready, she would take a pace, then pause and survey the cabin and the trees. Take a step and pause. Take a step and pause. She was on her fourth step, her left boot about to contact the ground, when she realized her mistake, when a startling insight flooded her mind. If there was a cleared space in front of the cabin, someone must have cleared it! Someone who used the cabin on a regular basis! And anyone who went to all the trouble to clear the vegetation around the door would hardly leave the cabin unattended with the door open! So if the door was open, then someone *must* be inside!

Bertha placed her left foot on the soil, intending to spin and race for cover. But she never made it. Her left boot touched the ground and didn't stop, sinking into the earth, into a gaping hole, almost spilling her off balance. She caught herself before she could plunge forward, and she was on the verge of pulling back from the edge of the hole when something slammed into the small of her back.

They had her.

Bertha received a fleeting glimpse of figures dashing from the cabin and the woods surrounding her, and then she pitched into the hole, into a large pit, crashing through a layer of dirt supported by a framework of branches and woven reeds and weeds.

Someone was laughing.

Bertha tried to clutch the rim of the pit, but her fingers slipped, unable to retain a purchase. She was aware of falling, of darkness, of dirt stinging her face and eyes, and then she landed with a jarring crash on her right side, the M-16 flying from her hands.

More laughter and giggling arose above her.

Stunned, Bertha rolled onto her back, gazing up at the rim of the pit seven feet away. Faces were looking down at her, but she couldn't focus on them. She shook her head, trying to correct her vision, and struggled to rise to her hands and knees.

"Not so fast, bitch!" shouted a harsh voice.

A hard object struck Bertha on the forehead, and she sprawled onto her face. Her last mental image before passing out was of Sundance.

8

"She should have been back by now," Blade declared, impatiently scanning the forest.

"Should we go look for her?" Sundance asked.

"You go," Blade said. "I'll stick with the SEAL. Take the autoloading rifle you brought from the Home with you."

Sundance twisted, leaned over, and retrieved his automatic rifle from the rear section. It was an outstanding piece of military hardware, an FN Model 50-63. The rifle featured a folding stock, an 18-inch barrel and 20-round magazine, and was chambered for the .308 cartridge. The FN 50-63 had initially been a semiautomatic, but the Family Gunsmiths had coverted it to full automatic. Next to his Grizzlies, Sundance preferred the FN over any other weapon in the massive Family armory.

"Be careful," Blade advised.

Sundance nodded, and exited the transport. He felt uncomfortable in the Russian uniform. The Grizzlies were in their shoulder holsters, nestled under the uniform shirt. He would need to unbutton the shirt to reach the Grizzlies, and he didn't like having them tucked away. Frowning, he hefted the FN and moved away from the SEAL. He had last seen Bertha walking to the west, and he hurried to a tree he remembered seeing her near.

There were her boot tracks, in the soft soil near the base of the tree.

Sundance searched the forest, then jogged to a thicket to the left of the tree. If Bertha had wanted privacy while she changed, the thicket would have screened her from the SEAL. He rushed to the far side of the thicket.

Bertha's Russian uniform was lying on the ground behind the thicket.

Sundance stopped, his penetrating green eyes sweeping the woods. Bertha was nowhere in sight. He grabbed her uniform and raced to the SEAL.

Blade was waiting for him outside the transport, standing near the front grill.

"I found this," Sundance announced as he approached, holding aloft the Russian uniform.

Blade took the uniform, scowling. He glanced at the woods.

"Do you want me to go look for her?" Sundance inquired.

"No," Blade replied.

"You're going to look for her?" Sundance asked.

"No," Blade said.

"We're not just going to leave her out there?" Sundance demanded, his tone rising.

"That's exactly what we're going to do," Blade stated.

"Like hell we are!" Sundance stated.

Blade stared at Sundance. "You'll do what I tell you to do."

Sundance gestured toward the trees. "But how can we just up and leave her? She could be in trouble! She could be counting on us to help her!"

"There's no doubt in my mind that she's in trouble," Blade said. "She wouldn't walk off and leave this uniform. But whatever fix she's in, she'll have to get out of by herself."

"Since when do Warriors desert their own?" Sundance asked bitterly.

"Normally, we don't," Blade said.

"Is this a special case?" Sundance queried.

"It is," Blade responded.

"You mind telling me in what way?" Sundance persisted.

Blade sighed. Sundance was obviously furious. "Our mission takes priority. Every run we go on, the mission is our primary consideration. We're under a time constraint on this run. We don't know if the Vikings the Russians captured are still alive, but we're operating under the assumption they are. Who knows what shape the Vikings are in after being questioned by the Soviets for over two weeks? We know the Reds don't go easy on their prisoners. The Vikings could be on their last legs."

Sundance opened his mouth to speak.

Blade held up his right hand. "I'm not finished. We know the Vikings were definitely in Philadelphia about two weeks ago. They could have been moved, but then again, they might still be there. In any event, the sooner we reach Philadelphia, the better."

"But Bertha—" Sundance began.

"I said I wasn't finished," Blade stated, cutting him off. "There's one more aspect to bear in mind. You're well aware of how close the Family came to being destroyed by the forces of the Doktor and the dictator ruling the Civilized Zone. You know we barely scraped through intact. And we could find ourselves in a similar situation real soon. The Soviets aren't to be trifled with. We might have strong allies in the Freedom Federation, but all of us combined are no more powerful than the Russians." Blade paused. "We have a chance here, Sundance, to turn the tide. If these Vikings are mortal enemies of the Russians, then we might be able to forge an alliance with them. The Soviets would be caught in a vise, between the Vikings on the east and the Freedom Federation in the west. Together, we might be able to defeat the Russians and drive them from the country." He paused again. "Knowing all of this, what do you think we should do about Bertha? Should we go after her? Where do we start looking?"

"Where I found the uniform," Sundance said.

"Okay. But we can't go waltzing through the forest yelling our lungs out for her. The Russians, or the damn mutants, might hear us and come to investigate. Which means we'd have to track her. Are you an expert tracker?"

"No," Sundance replied reluctantly.

"Neither am I," Blade said. "Geronimo is, but he isn't here. I'm a fair hand at it, but tracking takes time. Lots and lots of time. And time is the one thing we don't have to spare."

"I know," Sundance said, averting his eyes.

"I'd let you go after her," Blade stated, "but what if something happens to you? What then? I can't complete our mission by myself."

"And the mission is our primary consideration," Sundance quoted, his facial muscles tightening.

"Exactly," Blade affirmed.

"So we do nothing," Sundance snapped.

"We wait," Blade corrected him. "If she returns by nightfall, fine. If she doesn't, we leave for Philadelphia without her."

Sundance squinted up at the sun. "That doesn't give her much time."

"I know," Blade acknowledged.

Sundance studied his giant companion. "You know, I don't envy you."

"Don't envy me? Why?" Blade asked.

"I don't envy the responsibility you have," Sundance confessed. "I don't envy the decisions you must make. I don't think I'd ever want to be top Warrior."

Blade chuckled.

"What's so funny?" Sundance inquired.

"I was just thinking of something Hickok once said," Blade revealed.

"What did he say?"

"It was shortly after Hickok's son, Ringo, was born," Blade recalled. "Hickok said that being a Warrior is a lot like being a diaper."

"A diaper?" Sundance responded, surprised. "What in the world do Warriors and diapers have in common?"

Blade grinned. "We both get shit on a lot."

9

Ohhhhhh! Her aching head!

"She's comin' around!" a voice yelled.

Bertha slowly opened her eyes. Acute agony racked her, spreading from her forehead to her chin.

"She's awake!"

Bertha grit her teeth and turned her head, seeking the speaker. The last thing she remembered was falling into the damn pit. She found herself on a wooden table, flat on her back, her hands and feet securely bound. A sticky sensation prickled her forehead and face.

The table was surrounded.

There were over a dozen of them, kids of varying ages, boys and girls, all dressed in rags, all filthy.

Bertha blinked several times, wondering if she was dreaming. She could see a lantern hanging on a wall next to a closed door, and she realized she must be in the cabin.

"About time you woke up!" declared the oldest boy in the room. He was about 16, and wore a crudely fashioned, torn brown shirt and shredded jeans. His hair was red, his eyes green.

Bertha went to reply, but the mere act of moving her lips sparked an intense spasm in her head.

"I told you she's been hurt bad," said the eldest girl, a youth of 14 or 15 with stringy brown hair and brown eyes. She wore a patched, lopsided green shift.

"So what?" the oldest boy retorted. "Hunters are scum! She deserves what she got."

Bertha managed to elevate her head several inches from the table top. "Who . . . are you?" she mumbled.

The youngsters stepped back at the sound of her voice.

"Shut your mouth, Hunter!" the oldest boy barked.

"Hunter? I'm not hunting game," Bertha said. She closed her eyes as vertigo engulfed her.

"Game?" said one of the younger children, a girl of five or six. "Can we play a game?"

"Shut up, Milly!" the oldest boy ordered.

"Don't talk to Milly like that, Cole!" interjected the eldest girl.

"Butt out, Libby," Cole rejoined.

All of them began arguing at once, their commingled voices rising, filling the cabin with their clamorous dispute.

Bertha was too woozy to comprehend their squabbling. She rested her head on the table and closed her eyes. What was going on here? she asked herself. She'd been captured by a bunch of kids!

Someone prodded her on the left shoulder.

Bertha twisted to her left.

A young boy, not much over ten years of age, with long blond hair and big blue eyes, smiled at her. "Are you a Hunter?" he inquired in a high-pitched voice.

"I'm a Warrior," Bertha answered.

"What's a Warrior?" he wanted to know.

Bertha tried to answer, but her mouth refused to open. She grimaced as a throbbing twinge pierced her skull.

"What's a Warrior?" the boy repeated.

Bertha's eyelids fluttered, and she sank back, unconscious.

10

"What is it?" Sundance asked.

"Let's find out," Blade said.

Bright stars dominated the heavens. A cool breeze was wafting from the northwest. Before them, perhaps a hundred yards distant, was a huge archlike structure.

"I don't see any lights," Sundance whispered.

"Me neither," Blade commented. He moved toward the arch in a stooped-over posture, his Commando in his hands. The Commando Arms Carbine was one of his favorite guns. It came with an automatic or semi-automatic captibility, and only weighed about eight pounds. The Commando was about three feet in length, and used a 90-shot magazine. Blade had insured the magazine was fully loaded with 45-caliber ammunition before they had departed the SEAL. His last Commando had been lost in Chicago. Fortunately, there'd been another one in the extensive Family armory.

Somewhere off to the west an owl hooted.

Blade forced his mind to concentrate on the matter at hand. He was extremely worried about Bertha, and he couldn't allow his concern to affect his effectiveness.

They had waited at the SEAL until well after dark, with Sundance pacing back and forth the whole while, and Bertha had never appeared. Wherever she was, she was now on her own.

They reached a row of trees bordering the structure and stopped. Without the moon, the night was murky, and visibility was restricted. They could see for about ten yards; beyond that, only shadows.

Blade inched nearer to the arch. He discovered the ruins of a road and squatted, taking his bearings. They were traveling in a southerly direction, which meant the SEAL was parked in the forest about a mile to the north of the arch. The arch, whatever it might be, would serve as a landmark to guide them back to the SEAL. He glanced both ways, then sprinted to the base of the structure.

Sundance joined him.

The arch was rough to the touch, as if it had been constructed of stone. It rose high into the night, blocking out a section of the sky.

"What is it?" Sundance queried, running his left hand over the sandy texture.

"Maybe a monument of some kind," Blade deduced. "We studied about Valley Forge in school, remember?"

Sundance pondered for a moment. "Yeah. Didn't it have something to do with the Revolutionary War in America and George Washington, their first President?"

"This is the place," Blade affirmed. "This arch must be a memorial. Why else would they have put it in the middle of a field? I'm amazed it's still here after all this time."

Sundance motioned toward the field. "Didn't Bertha say this area was a park?"

"It was once," Blade said, "but I seriously doubt the Russians would have bothered to maintain a shrine to American liberty."

"Which explains why the place is overgrown with weeds," Sundance mentioned, "and why the road is a wreck."

"Let's go," Blade stated, leading off to the south.

They traversed another field and entered another stretch of woods.

"There's a light," Sundance said in a hushed tone, pointing.

Blade glanced to their left. A solitary light glowed approximately 400 yards to the southeast. "We'll take a look," he told Sundance.

The two Warriors bore to the southeast. The forest ended, and the Warriors discovered a quiet residential neighborhood. They crouched near a street curb and scanned the houses on both sides.

Blade felt his left Bowie hilt gouge his side. He had concealed the big knives under his uniform shirt, aligning the sheaths under his belt, with one Bowie on each hip. He shifted to alleviate the discomfort.

"Where is everyone?" Sundance murmured.

Blade was wondering the same thing. Except for the second residence on the left, all of the homes were dark, evidently uninhabited. And there was not a solitary soul in sight. He rose and ran across the street toward the first home on the left. The yard was a tangled jumble of weeds and brush, obviously neglected for years. Blade raced up the front porch, then stopped.

The home was a shambles, its door busted and hanging from the top hinge, its windows shattered. The pale yellow paint on the exterior was peeled and flaked.

Blade turned toward the next house. Sundance at his side, he jogged over to the north wall of the structure. The interior of the home was black, except for a flickering ball of light at ground level near the front door. The walls of this house, like the first, badly needed a paint job. Bits and pieces of broken glass from the windows lined the cement foundation.

The front door was located on the west side of the residence. Blade eased around the corner, bent down, and moved closer to the flickering light.

The glow was emanating from a busted basement window.

Blade dropped to his hands and knees, then inched to the edge of the window. He peeked past the metal lip.

The basement had a tenant. An elderly man with gray

hair and a long gray beard was seated on a wooden stool, hungrily gnawing on a roasted rabbit leg. A small fire was burning in the middle of the concrete floor. Dust and dirt covered the antique workbench, table, and chair positioned along the south wall, and the washer and dryer along the east wall. Cobwebs dotted the beams in the ceiling. A flight of stairs on the north side of the basement provided access to the first floor.

Blade examined the window, comparing its frame dimensions to the width of his shoulders. He decided he could do it.

Sundance was waiting behind him.

Blade twisted, motioned with his right arm toward the front door, then pointed at the basement window.

Sundance nodded his understanding. He crept past Blade and reached the door. The FN 50-63 in his left hand, he tried the doorknob with his right.

The door swung open with a slight creek.

Sundance grinned and disappeared inside.

Blade peered into the basement. The elderly man was still chewing on the rabbit leg, striving to strip every last vestige of meat from the bone. He wore a blue shirt and brown pants, both garments exhibiting more holes than fabric. His brown leather shoes qualified as relics; on both of them, his toes protruded from the ends.

Blade lowered himself onto his abdomen, then positioned his body so he was perpendicular to the window. He slowly counted to ten, and on the count of ten galvanized into action. Using his elbows, he slid his arms, head, and shoulders through the window. He aimed the Commando at the man eating the rabbit.

The man in the basement was almost as spry as the animal he was consuming. He was on his feet and darting for the stairs in an instant, but he halted after only five steps and raised his arms in the air, dropping the rabbit leg.

Sundance was standing on the stairs, the FN pointed at the elderly man's head.

Blade eased through the window, letting his body drop the seven feet to the floor. He executed an acrobatic maneuver in midair, jerking his feet down and swinging his torso upward, and alighted upright with the Commando trained on the man with the rabbit.

The elderly gentlemen glared from Sundance to Blade. "All right!" he snapped, displaying a gap where four of his upper front teeth had once been. "You caught me, you Commie bastards! Go on! Get it over with!"

Blade glanced at Sundance, who grinned.

"Get it over with!" the man demanded. "You finally caught old Nick! But it took you slime long enough, didn't it?" He cackled.

Blade walked toward the man called Nick. "What are you babbling about?" he asked.

Nick cocked his head and scrutinized the giant. "Damn! They're growin' you sons of bitches big nowadays, ain't they?"

'I think you're laboring under a misapprehension," Blade said.

Nick did a double take. "Damn! You pricks are speakin' better English all the time!"

"You have us confused with someone else," Blade stated.

"Oh? Who?" Nick replied.

"The Russians," Blade explained.

Nick laughed and shook his head, his beard swaying. "You morons! Do you really think old Nick is as gullible as that? I won't fall for your crock of shit!"

"We're not Russians," Blade said.

"You're not?" Nick responded in mock astonishment. "Then those must be ballet costumes you're wearin'!" He snickered.

Blade lowered the Commando barrel. "I'm serious. We're not Russians. We confiscated these uniforms."

"Yeah. Right. What are you tryin' to pull? Are you with the KGB?" Nick queried.

"What must I do to convince you we're not Russian troopers?" Blade inquired.

Nick tittered. "Sprout wings and a halo."

Blade indicated the smoldering fire with a wave of his left hand. "Why don't you have a seat? There are a few questions I'd like to ask you."

"I'll bet there are!" Nick declared, smirking. "I don't know what kind of game you're playin', but I'll go along with it. I don't have any choice, do I?"

Blade stepped aside as Nick walked to the stool and sat down. Sundance came down the stairs and moved to the right. He leaned against the wall, his automatic rifle cradled inis arms.

"I ain't never seen guns like yours," Nick mentioned, admiring the Commando in Blade's right hand.

"You see? Don't these guns prove we're not Russians?" Blade asked.

"They don't prove diddly," Nick retorted.

Blade sighed. "What are you doing down here all by yourself?"

"Jackin' off," Nick answered, and chuckled.

"Can't you give me a straight answer?" Blade queried.

"Why the hell should I?" Nick rejoined. "I hate all you Commie sons of bitches!"

"But I told you we're not Russians," Blade reiterated.

"Oh, you may not be from Russia," Nick said, "but you're still a Commie bastard! I know you're forcin' some of our women to have kids for you! I know you're raisin' the kids like they would have been raised in your rotten Motherland! I know!" His voice vibrated with the intensity of his emotion.

Blade frowned. This was getting them nowhere. He'd hoped to glean important information from their conversation, information which might aid Sundance and him in the attainment of their goal.

Sundance noted the expression on Blade's face. "Let's get out of here," he suggested. "This crazy old coot won't help us fight the Russians."

"I guess you're right," Blade admitted reluctantly. He smiled at Nick. "Be seeing you. Take care of yourself."

Blade and Sundance started toward the stairs.

Nick watched them cross the basement, his blue eyes narrowing suspiciously. "You're just gonna leave?"

"Yep," Blade confirmed.

"You ain't gonna kill me?"
"Nope," Blade answered.
"This is some kind of trick!" Nick exclaimed.
"Nope." Blade reached the bottom of the stairs.
"I don't get any of this," Nick muttered. "Why'd you bust in here, if you don't intend to kill me?"
Blade reached the third step. "I wanted to ask you a few questions."
"What questions?" Nick asked.
Blade paused. "You'll help us?"
"I still don't believe any of this," Nick said. "I think you're jerkin' me around. Then again, there's no way a pair of Hunters would walk off and let me live."
"Hunters?" Blade repeated.
"Don't tell me you don't know what Hunters are!" Nick stated.
"Of course we do," Sundance said. "Hunters kill game. I've hunted plenty of times. Deer, bear, ducks, you name it."
Nick squinted at Sundance. "Either you're the biggest idiot this world's ever seen, or you're the biggest liar."
Sundance turned. "I wouldn't make a habit out of calling me a liar."
"Touchy, ain't we?" Nick retorted.
"Will you help us?" Blade interjected.
Nick nodded. "You got me curious now. I'll answer your questions."
Blade and Sundance returned to the fire.
"So what are you doing down here all by yourself?" Blade asked again.
"Eatin' a rabbit I conked on the head with a rock," Nick said. "The homes around here were abandoned ages ago. I figured I could hide out here for a spell. No one ever comes around here, except the Hunters, of course. Valley Forge is off-limits."
"What are these hunters you keep talking about?" Blade inquired.
"Hunters are murderin' slime! The Commies train some of their soldiers in trackin' and night-stalkin', and everybody calls 'em Hunters. They hunt us down. Get a

bounty for every Freeb they kill. Double the bounty if its a Packrat,'' Nick detailed.

Blade's brow furrowed in perplexity. ''I don't understand. What's a Freeb? And a Packrat?''

Nick seemed surprised by the question. ''I'm a Freeb, dummy! And the Packrats are the kids, the ones hidin' out in Valley Forge.''

''You're a Freeb?'' Blade said. ''I still don't understand.''

Nick stared up at the giant, amused. ''They sure grow 'em stupid where you come from!''

''I told you we're not Russians,'' Blade stated sharply. ''And we're not from around here. We don't have the slightest idea what a Freeb is. Or a Packrat.''

Nick pursed his lips. ''You know, I'm beginnin' to believe you turkeys. Well, Freeb is short for freeborn. Anyone who ain't been printed and mugged by the Commies is called a Freeb 'cause the Commies ain't got no record of 'em. You understand that?''

''So far,'' Blade said. ''But why do the Russians mug people? To rob them?''

Nick gazed at the washer and dryer. ''Dummies! I'm dealin' with dummies here!''

''Who are you talking to?'' Sundance asked.

Nick pointed at the appliances. ''Them.''

Sundance glanced at Blade. ''This geezer is nuts.''

''*I'm* nuts?'' Nick said. ''Tell me somethin', boy. Do you know which end of a horse the shit comes out of?''

''Why are we dummies?'' Blade queried.

''Because you don't know what it means when I say the Commies mug folks. They take mug shots for their files. Get it? Photographs. Pictures. You do know what a photograph is?'' Nick said.

''I've seen some,'' Blade answered. Actually, he'd seen thousands. Kurt Carpenter had stocked the Family library with hundreds of volumes depicting a pictorial history of humankind. Photographic books on every subject were represented, from sailing to spaceships. ''But how is it you haven't been . . . printed and mugged . . . by the Soviets? Don't they mug everyone?''

''They try to,'' Nick stated. ''But they don't catch

everybody. Their Admin Centers are concentrated in the cities and towns, and they have trouble keepin' tabs on all the rural folks. I was born nearly seventy years ago, on a farm in western Pennsylvania. My mom and pop never took me in to be mugged."

"How long have you been hiding out like this?" Blade inquired.

Nick sighed. "Too damn long. I'm gettin' tired of all the runnin' and hidin'. I've been in these parts for about a year. There are a lot of abandoned homes around Valley Forge, and I keep movin' from one to the next. Like I said, no one ever comes here. It's illegal to be caught in Valley Forge. Oh, I bump into the Packrats now and again. But they keep their distance, and I keep mine. Besides, I ain't got nothin' they'd want."

"What are the Packrats?" Blade asked.

"The kids, dummy."

Blade looked at the window. "There are kids out there?"

"Bunches of 'em," Nick answered. "They live in gangs, and spend their time foragin' for food and fightin' each other. When they're not hidin' from the Hunters, that is."

"Where do these kids come from?" Blade queried.

"Everywhere," Nick replied. "But mostly from the big cities, like Philly. They're orphans, usually. Their parents get killed by the Commies, and they have nowhere else to go. So they hoof it. If they don't hit the road, the Commies will use 'em in their slave-labor camps. A lot of the runaways wind up here, or places like Valley Forge. They hear about it through the grapevine."

"Kids," Blade said, feeling an overwhelming revulsion for the Russians, and thinking about his little son Gabe.

"Don't feel sorry for 'em," Nick declared. "They're mean, the Packrats. They'd slit your throat for the clothes off your back. They trap folks from time to time, then torture 'em before they kill 'em."

"What happens to these kids when they grow up?" Blade asked.

"Few of 'em live that long," Nick said. "Those that do, just wander off to make a go of it someplace else."

Blade reached up and scratched his chin. "I know a lot of towns were evacuated during the war for one reason or another. Some were destroyed. So the map I have isn't completely reliable. And I need to know where the nearest inhabited town is located. What would it be?"

"King of Prussia is nearby," Nick revealed.

"Are there Russians there?" Blade queried.

"Commies? Why do you want to find the Commies?" Nick asked.

"We need to borrow one of their vehicles," Blade declared.

Nick chuckled. "You don't say! Well, in that case your best bet would be Norristown. The Commies have a large garrison stationed there. Where are you guys headed?"

"I'd rather not say," Blade said.

Nick shrugged. "No skin off my nose. This way, if I'm caught, I can't talk, huh?"

Blade nodded.

Nick stared from the giant to the one with the mustache. "You know, I may be gettin' senile, but I believe you two. I don't think you're Commies. No Commie could play dumb that good."

"Thanks," Blade said. "I think."

"Do you know where Norristown is?" Nick inquired.

"No," Blade replied. "We'll find it. I have a map with me."

"But the map won't tell you where the Commies like to post checkpoints, and which areas to avoid and which ones are safe." Nick silently debated for a minute. "Tell you what I'll do. I'll go along with you. Guide you. How about that idea?"

Blade shook his head. "It would be too dangerous."

"Dangerous?" Nick cackled. "I didn't live this long by takin' it easy, boy! Danger don't mean a thing to me."

"No," Blade said. He walked toward the stairs, Sundance at his side.

"I could show you some shortcuts," Nick persisted. "I know this area like the back of my hand."

Blade paused, reflecting. Since speed was of the essence, any shortcut would greatly facilitate their assignment. "Do you promise to do exactly as I tell you?" he asked.

Nick snickered. "Of course!"

"Then you can come," Blade said. "But only as far as Norristown. Once we've acquired a vehicle, you're on your own."

"I'm always on my own," Nick replied. He rose and hurried to the stairs. "Say! I never did catch your names."

"I'm Blade," Blade said introducing himself. "And this is Sundance."

"Sundance?" Nick chuckled. "Ain't never heard a name like Sundance before. What's your last names?"

"We don't have any," Blade answered.

Nick squinted at them. "No last names? Never heard of such a thing."

"Nobody has last names where we come from," Blade revealed.

"And where might that be?" Nick casually inquired.

"Sorry," Blade said. "We'd best keep that information to ourselves."

Nick shrugged. "Fine by me." He glanced from Blade to Sundance. "You know, I think we're goin' to have a real fun time together!"

11

Bertha slowly regained consciousness. She became aware of an acute pain in her wrists and arms. A cool breeze was blowing on her face. She could smell the fragrant scent of pine and dank earth. And she realized she wasn't on the table in the cabin; she was suspended by her wrists, her body dangling in the air.

What had happened?

Bertha opened her eyes, confirming her assessment. A rope secured her wrists. She glanced up, and found the rope was looped over the stout limb of a tree. Looking down, she discovered her feet were swaying about three feet above the ground. And she wasn't alone.

Six of the youngsters were facing her, three of them holding lanterns. The other three each held an AK-47.

Bertha recognized the oldest boy, the one called Cole. She also saw the girl with the stringy hair, Libby, and the little girl named Milly. The 10-year-old boy with the blonde hair was there, as was old Pudgy Butt himself, the brat who had led her into the trap. The other two she didn't know, a boy and a girl, both about 12 years old.

"Glad to see you joined us, bitch!" Cole greeted her.

Bertha glared down at him. Her headache had subsided, but her forehead was sore. "That ain't no way to talk to a lady, you snotnosed shithead!"

Cole bristled, leveling his AK-47 at Bertha's belly. "I should waste you right now, bitch!"

"While my hands are tied?" Bertha taunted him. "Ain't you the brave baby!"

Cole took a step toward her. "I'm not a baby!"

"Could of fooled me!" Bertha retorted.

Cole jammed the AK-47 barrel into her gut. "Damn you!"

"Cole! No!" The girl called Libby cried.

"Why not?" Cole demanded, glowering up at Bertha. "She's a damn Hunter! Who cares if it's quick or slow?"

Bertha remembered the squabble in the cabin. She glanced at Libby. "What's a hunter?"

"Don't you know?" Libby responded.

"Nope," Bertha said.

"Bullshit!" Cole exploded. "You expect us to believe you?"

Libby gazed at Cole. "She might be telling the truth."

"Are you going to let her trick you?" Cole snapped. "You know what the Hunters are like! They'll do anything to catch one of us! Lie! Wear disguises! Shoot us in the back! Anything!"

Libby stared at Bertha, her youthful face betraying her doubt.

Bertha recognized a possible ally in the girl. "Look. I ain't no lousy hunter! I'm a Warrior."

"What's a Warrior?" Libby asked.

"A Warrior protects others from harm," Bertha explained.

Cole laughed. "Can it, bitch! Nobody is going to believe a word you say!"

"I wasn't talkin' to you!" Bertha stated stiffly. "I was talkin' to Libby."

"You're not here to hurt us?" Libby inquired.

"Nope," Bertha answered.

Cole turned on Libby, waving his AK-47. "Come on, Libby! You're not falling for this shit, are you?" He spun toward Bertha. "If you're not here to harm us, then why'd you chase Eddy?"

"I thought he was in trouble," Bertha answered.

"Yeah! Right!" Cole rejoined.

Bertha looked at Eddy. "Didn't you attack me, Fatso?"

Eddy seemed confounded by the unexpected query.

"Didn't you attack me first?" Bertha prompted him. "Wasn't I mindin' my own business, and you jumped me from behind?"

"I wanted your gun!" Eddy blurted.

"And wasn't I turnin' back when you screamed?" Bertha asked.

"Yeah," Eddy admitted.

"There!" Bertha glanced at Cole. "I thought he was in trouble. If I'd wanted to waste Fatso, I could have shot him anytime!"

"It doesn't mean a thing!" Cole stated defiantly.

"Yes, it does," Libby chimed in.

"What?" Cole said.

"I believe her, Cole," Libby declared.

"Give me a break!" Cole quipped.

"I think she's telling the truth," Libby stated.

"Why?" Cole wanted to know.

"Lots of reasons," Libby said. "Have you ever seen a woman Hunter before?"

"No," Cole answered reluctantly.

"And have you ever seen a Hunter dressed like her?" Libby asked.

"No," Cole said, "but they wear all sorts of disguises!"

"What about her gun?" Libby pressed him. "Ever seen a Hunter packing a gun like hers?"

Cole's forehead creased. "No, can't say as I have. They always use an AK-47 or a pistol."

"And," Libby added triumphantly, pointing at their prisoner, "have you ever seen a *black* Hunter before? Ever *heard* of a black Hunter before?"

Cole slowly shook his head, studying the woman swinging from the rope.

"Cole . . ." said the little girl named Milly.

"Not now, Milly," Cole barked irritably.

"You finally seein' the light?" Bertha asked him.

"What's your name?" Cole inquired.

"Bertha."

"You gottta see it my way, Bertha," Cole said. "I'm the head of the Claws. Fifteen Packrats depends on me. If I make a mistake, they'll die."

"I'm not here to hurt you," Bertha reiterated.

"But I don't know that for sure," Cole mentioned. "If I go easy on you, cut you down, we could all wind up dead. I can't take the chance. Somebody is always after us. If it ain't the Red Hunters, then its one of the other Packrat gangs, or the mutants."

"Cole," Milly said, interrupting.

"Not now!" Cole told her. He gazed up at Bertha and shook his head. "Sorry, lady. But I can't let you live. You could be lying through your teeth for all I know. You could be some kind of new Hunter. We're just gonna have to leave you here for the mutants."

"Cole!" Milly cried.

Cole turned toward Milly, clearly annoyed. "Haven't I told you before not to butt in when I'm talking to someone else? What the hell is it now?"

Milly extended a trembling finger to their right.

"Eyes."

"Eyes?" Cole repeated, starting to pivot in the direction Milly was indicating.

Bertha glanced to the right, and she saw them first. A pair of reddish orbs, balefully staring at the youngsters from the stygian depths of the forest.

"A mutant!" Cole shouted. "Get to the cabin! Quick!"

The Claws responded to his order, dashing past Bertha toward the log cabin 20 yards away. One of them dropped a lantern.

Bertha glanced over her left shoulder and spotted the cabin, and saw Libby leading Milly and the others in a mad sprint for the cabin's front door. She swung her head around, just in time to see the mutant burst from cover and charge Cole.

The mutant was a canine, or would have been had its parents not been affected by the widespread chemical and radiation poisoning of the environment and given birth to a defective monstrosity. It was four feet high and covered with brown hair, and its features resembled those of a German shepherd. Its jaws slavering, its six legs pumping, its two tails curved over its spine, the mutant pounced.

Cole stood his ground. He crouched and fired, the stock of the AK-47 pressed against his right side. His shots were rushed, but effective.

The mutant staggered as the heavy slugs ripped into its body. It was wrenched to the right, but immediately recovered and renewed its attack.

Cole never let up. He kept firing as the mutant took a bounding leap, and he was still firing as the mutant slammed into him and knocked him to the ground.

The mutant recovered before Cole, and slashed at him with its tapered teeth.

Cole, flat on his back, brought the AK-47 up to block those cavernous jaws.

Enraged, the mutant clamped onto the AK-47, snarling as it strived to wrench the weapon from the human's hands.

Cole was clinging to the Ak-47 for dear life.

Bertha, suspended five feet from the savage struggle, saw her chance. She whipped her legs forward, then back. Once. Twice. Gaining momentum with each swing. And on the third try she tucked her knees into her chest, then lashed her legs out and down, hurtling at the combatants.

The mutant's senses were incredible. Furiously engaged as it was in attempting to tear the AK-47 loose and rip into its opponent's neck, it saw the woman sweeping toward it and tried to evade the blow. But in doing so, the mutant released the AK-47 and drew back, its head momentarily elevated.

In that instant, Bertha struck. Her black boots plowed into the mutant's face, into its feral eyes, and it was propelled for a loop, catapulted through the air to crash onto its left side six feet from Cole.

Cole took immediate advantage of the situation, rising to his knees, aiming the AK-47, deliberately going for the mutant's head, squeezing the trigger and holding it down.

The mutant twisted as it was struck, frantically scrambling erect. But the heavy slugs drove it to its knees, its left eye exploding in a spray of hair and blood. It reared back and howled as it was hit again and again and again.

The AK-47 went empty.

The mutant flopped onto its right side, its body convulsing. It whined once, then lay still.

Cole slowly stood, his eyes riveted on the mutant.

There was a commotion from the direction of the cabin, and the seven oldest Claws ran up, all of them armed.

"You got it!" shouted the pudgy Eddy.

Cole simply nodded.

Libby was with them, carrying an AK-47. She glanced at Cole, worry in her eyes. "It almost got you," she stated.

Cole exhaled loudly.

"You came close," Libby said.

"I know," Cole agreed in a soft voice.

"I saw the whole thing," Libby mentioned. "You'd

be dead right now, if she hadn't helped you!" And Libby pointed at Bertha.

Cole pivoted, gazed up at the Warrior.

"I couldn't let that freak eat you," Bertha said. "You might of given it indigestion!"

Cole almost grinned. He glanced at Eddy. "Cut her down."

"But I thought you said—" Eddy objected.

Cole whirled on the startled Eddy. "Cut her down! *Now*!"

"Thank goodness!" Bertha exclaimed. "I've really got to weewee!"

12

Blade had to hand it to Nick. The old Freeb was as good as his word. Nick seemed to know every alley, every ditch, every unfrequented street, within 20 miles of Valley Forge. His endurance and agility were remarkable for a man his age. He maintained a steady pace, never flagging, and they reached their destination two hours before dawn. They approached Norristown from the north. Nick guided them through the fields and across yards adjacent to Highway 363, then parallel to Egypt Road until they reached Ridge Pike. They continued to the south, sticking to the shadows, to the alleys and the side streets, skirting Jeffersonville, until they reached Norristown.

Blade was amazed by his first glimpse of Soviet-occupied territory. People appeared to be going about their daily business without hindrance. Traffic on the main arteries was light but steady. Civilian and military vehicles shared the roads. A checkpoint was posted between Jeffersonville and Norristown, but the Russians stationed at the checkpoint performed their duties in a desultory fashion. Squatting behind a hedgerow a block to the west, Blade saw the soldiers joking and laughing, and only occasionally stopping vehicles to verify papers. Again, he had to remind himself of the time frame involved. The Soviets had controlled this area for over 100 years. They were bound to be complacent after such a protracted interval. Which suited him fine, because their careless attitude increased the odds of successfully completing the run to Philadelphia.

Four times the trio inadvertently encountered civilians, and each time the civilians took one look at the Russian uniforms on Blade and Sundance and promptly made themselves scarce.

Once in Norristown, Nick increased their pace. They bore south on Lafayette, then turned left on Hawes Avenue, and dashed across Main Street to the far sidewalk. A military truck appeared in front of them, and Nick hastily led them into a side street. They traversed a succession of side streets and alleys, on the alert for patrols, until Nick abruptly stopped.

"There it is," the Freeb whispered.

They were standing at the end of a side street. Before them were railroad tracks, a wide avenue, and an imposing structure. Floodlights rimmed its roof. A barbed-wire fence enclosed the perimeter. Soldiers patrolled the length of the fence, some with guard dogs on a leash. A gate in the northwest corner of the fence was closed.

"What is it?" Blade asked.

"The Norristown garrison," Nick disclosed. "About eighty soldiers are headquartered there on a regular basis. There's a motor pool in the rear. The place used to be a newspaper. The *Times*-Something-or-Other. But the damn Commies took it over, like they did all the media."

"You know a lot about it," Sundance idly mentioned.

"You pick up bits and pieces here and there," Nick commented.

Blade was appraising the garrison's fortifications. "There's no way we can break in there to steal a vehicle."

"Maybe you won't have to," Nick said.

"What do you mean?" Blade inquired.

"Look," Nick said, pointing.

A guard was unlocking the gate in the northwest corner of the fence. He pushed the gate open and stepped aside, waiting. A moment later, a jeep drove around the corner of the garrison, evidently coming from the motor pool. The jeep braked at the gate, the driver exchanged a few words with the guard, and the jeep accelerated. It took a left.

"Hide!" Nick said, and before the Warriors understood his intent, he moved from the cover of the side street, out into the open, in clear view of the jeep's driver.

Blade grabbed Sundance's right arm, and they retreated into the shadows.

"What's he doing?" Sundance queried.

"I think I know," Blade said.

Nick was wobbling on his feet, staggering, seemingly inebriated. He glanced at the jeep, then put his left hand in the crook of his right elbow and snapped his forearm up, his right hand clenched into a fist.

The jeep slowed, then swerved, wheeling toward Nick.

Nick laughed and backpedaled, tottering.

The jeep was bearing down on the side street.

Nick stayed on the sidewalk, stumbling away from the wide avenue, leading the jeep further up the side street, out of sight of the garrison gate.

The jeep screeched to a stop, and two Russian soldiers climbed out, leaving the vehicle running.

"Hey, you bloodsuckers!" Nick called and snickered.

"Hello, comrade," the driver greeted Nick. He was stocky, his complexion florid.

"I ain't your lousy comrade!" Nick retorted.

"You are drunk, comrade," stated the second Russian.

Nick laughed. "What was your first clue, butthole?"

The driver and the other Russian exchanged glances. "You will need to come with us," the driver said.

"Like hell I will!" Nick rejoined belligerently.

"You must come with us, comrade," the driver persisted.

"Why?" Nick inquired.

The driver and the second soldier walked toward the old man. They believed he was intoxicated, harmless, and in one respect they were correct. But in another, they were wrong.

"Please," the driver said, "do not resist! Public drunkenness is not permitted."

Nick straightened. "What about dyin'?"

The driver detected a movement to his left, and he spun, going for the automatic pistol on his right hip. His fingers were closing on the grips when other fingers clamped onto his neck. Powerful fingers, with a grip of steel. He caught a glimpse of a giant in uniform, and then he was bodily lifted from the sidewalk.

The second trooper saw the giant spring on the driver, and he went for his own gun.

Sundance sprang from the shadows, his arms swinging the FN barrel up and around, ramming the barrel into the second soldier's throat. The soldier gagged, doubling over, and Sundance smashed the barrel against his head twice in swift succession. The soldier gasped and fell to his knees. Sundance drew back his right leg, then planted his right foot on the tip of the soldier's chin. The soldier flipped onto his back, blood spurting from his crushed teeth, oblivious to the world. Sundance glanced at Blade.

The head Warrior, his Commando slung over his left shoulder, was holding the driver's neck in his right hand and the driver's midsection in his left, while supporting the trooper in the air above his head. The Russian was kicking and wheezing, his brown eyes bulging. Blade suddenly brought his massive arms straight down, and the driver's head produced a sickening crunching sound as it struck the sidewalk.

"Nice job," Nick complimented them.

Blade glanced at the mouth of an alley 20 yards off. "Let's stash them in there," he suggested. Suiting action to words, he stooped over and gripped the driver by the collar. "Hurry."

The two Warriors hastily deposited the soldiers in the

alley, secreting the Russians behind a row of trash cans.

"That should do it," Blade said. "Let's get out of here."

Blade and Sundance jogged to the idling jeep. As Blade was about to slide in, he stopped and looked around. "Where's Nick?"

Sundance swiveled. "I don't see him," he said.

"Damn!" Blade spat in annoyance. What the hell had happened to the Freeb? "We can't wait!" He eased into the jeep.

"Move it, dummy!" declared a voice from the rear.

Blade twisted.

Nick was hunched over in the narrow back seat. "You'd best take off! We've been lucky so far! I didn't see anyone lookin' out their window. Haul ass before we're spotted!"

Sundance climbed into the jeep.

"We can't take you with us," Blade said to Nick.

"What's with you?" Nick demanded. "One second you're actin' like you're goin' to piss your pants because you can't find me, the next you're bootin' me out on my can."

"I told you before," Blade reminded the Freeb. "We agreed you could come with us as far as Norristown and that was it."

Nick leaned forward. "I didn't agree to nothin! And I haven't had this much fun in years! I'm comin' with you, unless you up and toss me out. And you'd best get your ass in gear. Someone's liable to peep out at us at any moment. And that Commie on the gate might be wonderin' what happened to this jeep."

Blade glanced at Sundance.

"Bring him," Sundance recommended. "He might come in handy."

Blade, annoyed, executed a tight U-turn and drove to the wide avenue. True to Nick's prediction, the gate guard was standing near the northwest corner, gazing in their direction. Blade waved at the guard, hoping his features were invisible in the dark interior of the jeep.

"That's a nice touch," Nick commented. "He'll think you're his buddy."

Blade took a right.

"Don't forget to stop at the red light," Nick stated.

Blade braked at the first intersection.

"So where are we goin'?" Nick asked.

Blade sighed. "Philadelphia."

"Philly?" Nick chuckled. "I know Philly like the back of my hand."

"I thought you would," Sundance interjected, grinning.

"What's in Philly?" Nick inquired.

Blade twisted and glared at the Freeb.

"Fine," Nick remarked. "I can take a hint. Go straight."

The light turned green, and Blade drove straight.

"Don't worry about a thing," Nick said. "I'll direct you to the turnpike, and we'll be in Philly before you know it."

"How long will it take?" Blade asked.

"We should be there by dawn," Nick replied. "Of course, it would help if I knew exactly where you want to go."

"I'm not exactly sure," Blade confessed.

"Oh, that's brilliant!" Nick scoffed. "You go to all the trouble of infiltratin' the Commie lines, you swipe one of their jeeps, and you don't know where the hell you want to go? What do you boys use for brains? Sewage?"

Blade's hands tightened on the steering wheel. He felt uncomfortable for several reasons. First, he didn't like having Nick along. But the elderly Freeb had served them well, so far, and he might really know Philadelphia like the back of his hand. Secondly, he felt awkward driving the jeep. He'd used a vehicle with a manual shift before, when he'd driven some of the trucks and jeeps the Family had appropriated during the war with the Doktor and Samuel II. But he usually drove the SEAL, and the vast difference was oddly discomfiting. Finally, a vague, worrisome sensation was nagging at his mind. Something was subliminally bothering him, and he was peeved because he couldn't isolate and identify the reason.

"Don't you have a clue what you're lookin' for?" Nick queried.

"Did you happen to hear about an attack on—" Blade began.

"Those hairy weirdos in the wooden ships?" Nick exclaimed. "Yeah. Everybody was talkin' about 'em for a while. They had the Commies pretty rattled, I heard."

"I'll bet," Sundance commented. He gazed out the rear window.

"So what about 'em?" Nick asked.

"We want to find them," Blade said, then elaborated. "We know the Soviets captured twelve of those invaders, those Vikings. We know the Russians are holding them at a detention facility in Philadelphia. And we want to find them."

"How'd you learn all this?" Nick inquired.

"That'll have to be our secret," Blade responded.

"Well, I don't know as I can be of much help," Nick said. "I don't have the slightest idea where the Commies are holdin' the ones you want."

"Do you know where they might be held? Where the detention facilities are located?" Blade probed.

Nick contemplated for a minute. "I might be of some help, after all. I know the Commies built a big detention place in northwest Philly, in Fairmont Park, right off the Schuykill Expressway. It's near the Schuykill River."

"Then we'll try there first," Blade said.

"I don't get it," Nick stated. "What are these Vikings to you guys?"

"Nothing," Blade answered.

"Then why do you want to find them?" Nick asked.

Sundance twisted in his seat. "You sure are the curious type, aren't you?"

Nick shrugged. "Sorry. Didn't mean to be nosy."

Sundance jerked his thumb toward his window. "What was that bridge we just went over?"

"It goes over the Schuykill River," Nick revealed.

"The same river near the detention facility?" Blade queried.

"Yep."

"Any chance of us following the river into Philadelphia?" Blade inquired.

"Nope."

"Why not?" Blade pressed.

"Because the roads don't follow the Schuykill, dummy," Nick disclosed. "Our best bet would be to take the Schuykill Expressway all the way in. It sticks close to the river most of the way."

"Can you direct us there?" Blade asked.

"No problem," Nick asserted.

"We do have one problem," Sundance remarked.

"Oh? What's that?" Blade replied.

"We're being tailed," Sundance said.

Blade glanced in the rearview mirror. A pair of headlights was in their lane, perhaps 500 yards distant.

"They pulled out of the garrison as we were going over the bridge," Sundance said. "They didn't even stop for a red light at the intersection."

Nick chuckled. "Sharp eyes you've got there, Sundance."

Sundance looked at Nick. "I don't miss much."

"We've got to lose them," Blade stated.

"Whatever we're going to do," Sundance declared, "we'd better do quickly."

"Why?" Blade asked.

Sundance was gazing over his left shoulder. "Because they're gaining on us."

13

"You should get some sleep," Bertha said.

"I'm too excited to sleep!" Libby stated happily.

"Me, too," Cole added.

They were seated at the wooden table in the cabin, a lantern in the center of the tabletop diffusing a soft yellow light throughout the room. The rest of the Claws were asleep, curled up on blankets on the floor.

"Do you really think they'll take us?" Libby queried in a low voice.

"They took me, didn't they?" Bertha replied. "Believe me, girl. The Family are the nicest bunch of folks you'd ever want to meet. We may have to cram the SEAL to the max, but Blade will agree to take you to the Home. I promise you."

"This Blade you've been telling us about," Cole said. "What's he like?"

"He's a righteous dude," Bertha stated. "One of my best friends. He's got more muscles than anyone else I know. And he's tricky."

"Tricky?" Cole repeated.

"I don't know how else to describe him," Bertha said. "He doesn't look like the brainy type, but he fools you. Just when you think you've got him figured out, he catches you off guard. I guess clever is the word for Blade."

"I'm looking forward to meeting him," Cole said.

Libby scanned the sleeping Claws. "But will there be enough room in this SEAL of yours for all of us?"

Bertha surveyed the children. "I don't know," she acknowledged. "We might need to throw out some of our supplies. But we'll find a way. Trust me."

Libby stared at Bertha. "I haven't trusted anyone for years."

Bertha frowned. "How do you make a go of it? Where do you find your food?"

"We do a lot of hunting and fishing," Cole detailed. "And we steal whatever we can get our hands on. We raid the nearby houses. Scrounge here and there."

Bertha nodded at a row of eight AK-47's leaning against the wall near the front door. "Where'd you get all the hardware?"

"Hunters," Cole answered.

Bertha whistled. "You Claws must be real good if you wasted that many Hunters."

"We get lots of practice," Cole stated. "They send in about a Hunter a month." He paused. "Funny."

"What is?" Bertha asked.

"The Hunters," Cole said. "Why do the fucking Russians only send in a Hunter at a time? Why not send in an army, and clean up Valley Forge in one day? And why do the Hunters only kill one Packrat, then split?"

"What?" Bertha leaned on her elbows on the table.

"That's what they do," Cole clarified. "They rack one Packrat, then leave. Four months ago Milly and Tommy were out picking berries. A damn Hunter popped up and blasted Tommy. Then he walked over to Milly, tickled her under the chin, and left."

"Why would he do that?" Bertha queried in surprise.

"Cole has an idea," Libby said.

"What is it?" Bertha prompted Cole.

The Claw leader gazed fondly at the slumbering Claws. "I think the Russians are using us as some kind of training exercise for their soldiers. I don't think they want to wipe us out. I think they're playing games with us, killing us off one at a time. Hell! They know we're here! And they don't usually let rebels keep on living. I know! They butchered my father and mother because my parents hated their guts!"

Bertha considered the theory. In a perverse sort of way, it made sense. The Russians knew the orphaned, homeless kids were flocking to Valley Forge, yet did nothing to stop the influx. Cole had said earlier that the Russians used disguises, even befriended some of the Packrats before slaughtering them. Why else would the Soviets go to so much trouble, unless the soldiers, probably their top commandoes, were honing their deadly skills on the lives of the Packrats? She stared at Cole with new respect.

"If we can get them out of here," Cole said, motioning toward the Claws, "I'll be the happiest man alive."

Bertha almost laughed at his use of the word "man." She stopped herself, though. Cole's parents, as Plato would say, had passed on to the higher mansions. Rather than submit to the Soviets, Cole had opted to resist. And now he was responsible for the lives of 15 others, for insuring they didn't starve to death and weren't killed by the Hunters, the mutants, or other

Packrats. Perhaps he did qualify as a man, after all. "How many other Packrat gangs are there in Valley Forge?" she asked him.

"Four I know of," Cole replied. "Maybe a few more. We each have our own turf to protect. The Bobcats are the closest to us, to the south a ways. We have run-ins with them all the time."

"Why don't all of you band together?" Bertha inquired. "There's strength in numbers."

"Band together?" Cole said. "I don't know. No one's ever thought of it, I guess. Besides, everybody shoots first and asks questions later. If I tried to make the peace with, say, the Bobcats, I'd be shot before I could even open my mouth."

"Sounds to me like you Packrats are playin' into the Soviets' hands," Bertha mentioned.

"There's nothing I can do about it," Cole stated. "It's been this way since before I came here."

"How long have you been here?" Bertha asked.

"Three years," Cole answered. "I wandered into Valley Forge after splitting from Phoenixville."

"How'd you hook up with the Claws?" Bertha probed.

"They were the first Packrats to find me," Cole said. "That's the way it usually works. Strays are taken in by the first group they come across."

Bertha shook her head. "I'm telling you! You bozos would do a lot better if you got organized. I used to belong to a gang in the Twin Cities, and I know what I'm talkin' about."

"You were in a gang?" Libby asked.

"Shhhhh!" Cole abruptly hissed.

Bertha glanced at the windows. Daylight was still an hour or two away, and the forest outside was shrouded in inky gloom.

"What is it?" Libby queried nervously.

Cole turned in his wooden chair and stared at the closed door. "I don't know. I thought I heard something."

"Could one of the other gangs, like the Bobcats, be sneakin' up on you?" Bertha inquired.

Libby shook her head. "No one goes out in the woods at night. It's too dangerous. The Packrats always hole up after dark."

"What about the Hunters?" Bertha remarked.

"Sometimes they come after us at night," Libby revealed. "But not often."

"Shhhh!" Cole shushed them. He stood and walked to the left window, cautiously standing to the right of the glass and peering out.

"Anything?" Libby asked in a whisper.

"No," Cole whispered back.

"I'll go have a look," Bertha proposed, rising. Her M-16 was propped against her chair. She grabbed it and moved to the doorway.

"If anyone's going out there, it'll be me," Cole said.

"I can take care of myself," Bertha informed him, her left hand on the doorknob. "You stay put and watch your Packrats."

"Bertha!" Libby said.

Bertha hesitated. "What?"

"Be careful!" Libby advised. "We can't afford to lose you! Not now!"

"Nothin' will happen to me," Bertha assured her. She opened the door, stepped outside, then closed it.

A strong wind was blowing in from the west, rustling the leaves on the trees. Above the cabin stars were visible.

Bertha faced into the wind, enjoying the cool tingle on her skin. She was feeling fatigued, and was glad dawn was not far off. Cole, Libby, and the rest could go with her to the SEAL. She hoped Blade and Sundance were still there.

A twig snapped.

Bertha was instantly on guard, warily raising the M-16 and searching the woods for an intruder, human or otherwise. She advanced toward the trees, bypassing the re-covered pit near the front door. The light from the cabin windows provided a faint glow to the edge of the trees. Bertha reached the tree line and stopped, crouching.

The wind was whipping the limbs, creating a subdued

clatter, mixed with the creaking of branches and the swishing of leaves.

Bertha strained her senses.

An audible scraping arose from the forest directly ahead.

Was it two limbs rubbing together? Bertha craned her neck and tilted her head, believing she could hear better.

Instead, she exposed her neck to the unseen lurker in the woods. A rope suddenly snaked out of the darkness, and a loop settled over her head and neck. Before she could react, Bertha was hauled from her feet and onto her stomach, the loop tightening about her neck, forming a noose, even as whoever was on the other end of the rope gave it a tremendous tug.

Bertha landed with the M-16 underneath her abdomen. She rolled, expecting her assailant to charge, but her attacker had another idea. The rope was yanked taut, and it felt like her head was being wrenched from her neck. Her breath was cut off, and she gagged as she struggled to her knees and released the M-16, clutching at the noose, her fingers urgently striving to pry the rope loose.

A burly man burst from cover, a 15-inch survival knife in his right hand, the rope in his left. He was dressed all in black, and his head was covered with a black mask. The knife extended, he rushed from behind a tree five yards away.

Damn! Bertha knew he had been waiting for her to drop the M-16! She let go of the rope and dived for the M-16, but her foe was already upon her.

The man in black launched his hefty body into a flying tackle, dropping the rope, and his left arm caught Bertha around the neck and drove her back, her desperate fingers inches from the M-16, and slammed her to the ground, onto her back, with him on top of her.

Bertha grunted and jerked her head to the right, and the survival knife plunged into the ground next to her left ear.

The man in black swept the knife up for another blow.

Bertha bucked and heaved, unbalancing her opponent, causing him to teeter to the right. She brought her right fist up and cuffed him on the cheek.

The man in black slashed at her face.

Bertha turned her face aside, but felt the keen edge of the survival knife slice open her right cheek.

The man stabbed at her right eye.

Bertha narrowly evaded the knife. Her left hand clutched his right wrist and held on fast.

He clamped his left hand on her throat.

Bertha was in dire straits. She was tiring, and tiring rapidly. She needed to do something, *anything,* to gain the advantage, or she was lost. Her years of street fighting served her in good stead. She jabbed her right hand upward, burying her forefinger in her attacker's left eye.

The man in black yelped, and his grip on her throat slackened.

Exerting her strength to its limits, Bertha surged her hips and stomach off the ground, tumbling the assassin over her head. She scrambled to her hands and knees, twisting to confront her foe.

He was superbly trained. Even as he landed on the dank earth, the man in black tumbled, coming out of the roll and straightening, whirling toward the woman in green.

The cabin door unexpectedly opened, spilling more light outside, bathing Bertha and the man with the survival knife.

The man in black spun, anticipating a threat from the cabin. For a fleeting moment, his back was to Bertha.

In a twinkling, Bertha struck. She shoved off from the ground, bringing her right foot up and around, executing one of the karate kicks taught to her by Rikki-Tikki-Tavi, the Family's supreme martial artist. It was a basic roundhouse kick, a Mawashi-geri, and it connected with the man in black between his shoulder blades.

The man in the mask was knocked forward by Bertha's kick. He tripped and toppled onto the makeshift latticework covering the pit. The limbs and reeds rent with a resounding crash, and the man in black sank into the pit.

Cole ran from the cabin, a lantern in his left hand, an AK-47 in his right. He halted at the pit rim.

Bertha saw the fury on Cole's features, and she surmised his intent at one glance. "Cole! No!" she shouted.

To no avail.

"Here, bastard!" Cole barked, and squeezed the trigger.

Bertha froze in midstride. She looked down, unable to prevent the inevitable.

The man in black was just scrambling to his feet when the slugs plowed into his chest and flung him against the pit wall. His body twitched and thrashed as more and more rounds were poured into him. A linear pattern of crimson geysers erupted across his torso, then angled higher, stitching a red path from his chin to the top of his head. The firing ceased, and the man in the mask pitched onto his face.

Cole gazed at his handiwork, smirking.

"You didn't have to do that!" Bertha exclaimed, panting.

Cole glanced at her. "Yes, I did."

"We could of questioned him!" Bertha stated. "He was a Hunter, right?"

"Without a doubt," Cole said.

Bertha doubled over, her ribs aching. "You didn't have to do that!" she reiterated.

Cole stared at the startled Claws emerging from the cabin, a few rubbing their sleepy eyes. He looked at Bertha, the set of his jaw determined and straight, and then at the corpse in the pit. "Yes, I did," he insisted softly.

This time, Bertha didn't argue.

14

"What the hell are they trying to pull?" Blade snapped.

"Beats me," Sundance admitted.

"Maybe they weren't after us at all," Nick commented.

The headlights behind them, after trailing the jeep for several miles, had turned off the highway.

"I don't get it," Blade said. "First, they almost catch up to us. Then they fall back and follow us for a while. Now, they're taking off. It doesn't make any sense."

"Who said the damn Commies have to make sense?" Nick asked.

Blade sighed. He was still experiencing a premonition of danger. But why?

"Take a left up ahead," Nick directed. "Stick with me, boys, and old Nick will guide you right up to the detention facility's front door."

"You'd do that for us?" Sundance queried.

"Hey! What are friends for?" Nick remarked light-heartedly. He patted Blade on the back. "Right, Warrior?"

And suddenly Blade recognized the source of his apprehension. The trifling inconsistencies accumulated into a plausible explanation, the only explanation possible under the circumstances. He smiled at Nick in the rearview mirror. "Right, Freeb," he replied.

Nick grinned. "Glad to see you're comin' around to my way of thinkin'!"

"I may be slow," Blade said, "but I catch on eventually." He glanced at Sundance.

Sundance grinned and nodded. "About time."

Blade realized Sundance had beaten him to the punch. How? What were the clues he had missed?

They drove to the southeast, Blade heeding Nick's infallible directions, using back roads until they reached the Schuykill Expressway.

"Just follow this south," Nick instructed them once

they were on the Expressway. "We'll be there before you know it."

"I can hardly wait," Blade mentioned. There were few vehicles on the road at such an early hour, and he maintained the speed at 50 miles an hour. Twice military transports passed on the opposite side of the Expressway traveling to the north.

"Look for the City Line exit," Nick advised.

"Will do," Blade stated.

The jeep reached the specified exit within minutes.

Blade wheeled onto City Line Avenue, moving to the southwest. A bakery truck approached from the other direction, conducting its morning deliveries.

"You want to make a left on Belmont Avenue," Nick disclosed.

Blade did, and a sign loomed ahead.

"The Vladimir I. Lenin Ministry of Psychological Sciences," Sundance read aloud. "Two miles."

"That's it!" Nick declared. "That's the place you want!"

"That's the detention facility?" Blade queried.

"That's it," Nick confirmed.

"You're sure?" Blade persisted.

"Of course I'm sure!" Nick retorted, annoyed. "Have I lied to you yet?"

Sundance began scratching at his chest. He idly started unbuttoning his uniform shirt.

Blade glanced over his right shoulder. "I doubt I could count all the lies."

Nick bristled angrily. "What the hell are you ravin' about?"

"Just this," Sundance stated, spinning in his seat, a gleaming Grizzly in his right hand.

Nick's eyes widened. "Hold on there, boy! What is this?"

"You tell us," Blade said.

"I don't know what you're talkin' about," Nick averred.

Blade looked at Sundance. "Why don't you do the honors?"

"Gladly," Sundance agreed. He leaned toward Nick.

"If you don't cut the crap, right now, I'm going to plant a bullet right between your eyes."

Nick was gawking from Sundance to Blade in bewilderment.

"The next words out of your mouth better be truthful ones," Sundance warned. "What's your real name?"

Nick's shoulders slumped. "Georgii Bakunin."

"Your rank?"

Bakunin frowned. "Captain."

"You're out of uniform, aren't you, Captain?" Sundance asked sarcastically.

Bakunin motioned with his left hand toward his face. "May I?"

"Only if you do it *real* slow," Sundance cautioned. "Twitch the wrong way and you're history."

Bakunin slowly raised his left hand and gripped the top of his long gray beard. He tugged on the upper right corner and his "beard" flopped to the floor.

"What about the hair?" Sundance queried.

"Dyed," Bakunin revealed. He ran his hand over his face, removing his "wrinkles."

"And the missing teeth?" Sundance said.

Bakunin reached his fingers into his mouth, scraping and pulling, and a minute later extracted a gummy black substance. His four upper front teeth miraculously reappeared.

"Pretty clever," Sundance conceded.

"What did I do wrong?" Bakunin asked in a pained tone.

"You figure it out for yourself," Sundance said.

"I'd like to know," Bakunin stated.

Sundance wagged the Grizzly barrel. "Don't press it. I'll pose the questions. What were you doing in that abandoned house?"

"Waiting for Packrats," Bakunin answered.

"You're a Hunter," Sundance deduced.

Bakunin nodded.

"You kill kids for a living," Sundance growled.

"No!" Bakunin said hastily. "It's required for all officers in Elite Branch."

"There's something I'd like to know," Blade interrupted, concentrating on his driving. "Why'd you string us along? Why'd you help us get this far? Why didn't you turn us in back at the garrison in Norristown?"

"I wanted to discover the reason you were here," Bakunin explained. "Find out what your connection to the Vikings might be."

"So you let us jump your comrades in Norristown," Sundance commented. "Didn't it bother you, knowing they could be hurt, or worse?"

"We must all make sacrifices for the cause," Bakunin said.

"The cause?" Sundance repeated quizzically.

"For the greater glory of Communism," Bakunin stated proudly.

"How did you know we were Warriors?" Blade interjected.

"You told—!" Bakunin started to reply, then angrily smacked his right palm against his forehead. "What an idiot I've been!"

"I wouldn't say you're an idiot," Sundance said. "Stupid, maybe, but not a complete idiot."

"How did you know we were Warriors?" Blade repeated his question.

Bakunin stared at the giant Warrior. "Your name was vaguely familiar. Something about it rang a bell. And then I remembered the incident in Washington, the one involving another Warrior named Hickok, I believe. And I recalled seeing an intelligence report on your Family."

"The information the spy in Denver uncovered," Blade speculated.

"We have a spy in Denver?" Bakunin asked innocently.

"What did this intelligence report say?" Sundance queried.

"It was merely a brief rundown on your Family," Bakunin replied. "A capsule summary of your Family's known history, organization, and leadership. It included a section on the Warriors, and contained a paragraph on the head of the Warriors. A man of gigantic proportions. A man named Blade."

Another sign materialized ahead, displaying an arrow indicating the direction they should travel to reach the Ministry of Psychological Sciences.

Blade took a left.

"Uh-oh," Sundance commented.

Five hundred yards to the southeast was a huge stone wall, 15 feet in height, capped with another 4 feet of barbed wire. A latticed iron gate, now closed, provided the only means of entering the Ministry. Four soldiers stood outside the gate.

Blade spotted a turnoff to the right and took it. The jeep lurched as he spun the steering wheel sharply, and then they were on a quiet side road. A stand of trees and brush screened the jeep from the guards at the iron gate. He braked the jeep.

"Now what do we do?" Sundance inquired.

"We proceed with the mission," Blade said.

"But how do we know this jerk was telling the truth about this place?" Sundance asked. "How do we know it's even a detention facility? Bakunin never said the Vikings were here for sure."

Blade glanced at the Russian. "No, he didn't. But so far, all the directions he's supplied have been right on the mark. Oh, he lied about who he was and lied to gain our confidence. But he told the truth about the garrison in Norristown, and about how to get to Norristown from Valley Forge. He didn't want us to know he was a soldier, didn't want us to discover his secret before he discovered ours, so he gave us accurate directions, expecting us to trust him, hoping we would blurt out the information he wanted. He couldn't come right out and say he definitely knew where the Vikings were being held, because that would have been too obvious, too suspicious. But he could, and did, give us a viable lead. I could be wrong, but I think he was telling the truth about the Ministry. The Vikings might well be there."

Sundance nodded toward Bakunin. "What do we do about him?"

Blade studied the captain. The wisest recourse was to kill Bakunin and dump his body in the weeds. Leaving the Russian alive needlessly invited trouble. If they tied him up, Bakunin might escape and alert the Ministry guards. A true expert could always slip free of constraints if given enough time. Blade seriously considered slitting Bakunin's throat, but then his conversation with Plato concerning excessive brutality flashed through his mind and he frowned. "We'll tie him up," he stated.

"You're the boss," Sundance said, "but if it was up to me, I'd waste the son of a bitch right now."

Blade nodded. "I agree with you."

"What? Then why are we going soft on him?" Sundance responded in surprise.

"It's something Plato said," Blade revealed. "About us not stooping to their level."

"Plato isn't a Warrior," Sundance stated cryptically.

Blade knew Sundance was right, but he didn't want to debate the issue. His affection for his mentor overrode his seasoned inclination. Just this once, he told himself, he'd do it Plato's way. Give Plato's outlook a chance. And hope he wouldn't live to regret it.

But he did.

"We don't have any rope," Sundance mentioned.

"We'll improvise," Blade said. He slid his right Bowie from under his shirt.

"What's that for?" Bakunin asked when he saw the big knife.

"I thought I'd carve my name on your forehead," Blade quipped. He shifted in his seat, examining its fabric. The back of the seat was covered by a leather-like, durable material. He inserted his knife into the fabric and began slicing wide strips from the seat.

"Cup your hands together and hold your arms out toward Blade," Sundance directed the captain.

Bakunin complied.

Blade swiftly bound the Russian, applying the strips to the officer's wrists and ankles, cutting additional strips as needed.

"You are cutting off my circulation," Bakunin said at one point.

"Should we cry now or later?" Sundance retorted.

Blade applied two strips around Bakunin's mouth,

effectively gagging the Soviet officer. "This should keep you comfy until we return." He eased his Bowie under his shirt.

Bakunin's eyes were simmering pools of hatred.

Blade accelerated, seeking another turnoff. He found a field after driving 60 yards, an overgrown patch of weeds and brush to his left, and he angled the jeep into the densest undergrowth. He stopped when he was satisfied the jeep was concealed from passersby on the road. "This will suffice," he announced, and switched off the ignition, placing the keys in his right front pants pocket.

Sundance replaced his Grizzly under his shirt. "What's our first move?" he queried as he buttoned up.

"We'll see how close we can get to that wall," Blade said. "Check out the layout."

Sundance grabbed his FN 50-63 and exited the jeep.

Blade verified the strips binding Bakunin were tight, then patted the captain on the head. "I want to thank you for your assistance. We couldn't have done it without you." He chuckled.

Bakunin vented his anger in a string of expletives, his words muffled by the gag.

"Be nice," Blade baited him. "And make yourself right at home. We'll be back in a bit." He climbed from the jeep, clutching the Commando in his right hand.

Sundance was waiting at the front of the vehicle.

Blade took the lead, moving off into the brush, heading for a row of trees close to the wall. Bright lights were discernible through the trees.

A tinge of faint light rimmed the eastern horizon.

"We'll have to hurry!" Blade remarked. "Dawn isn't far off."

Sundance nodded.

The two Warriors jogged to the row of trees and took cover behind two maple trunks, Sundance to Blade's right.

Blade peered around the bole of the tree, scanning the landscape ahead.

A field, 20 yards in width, separated the trees from the stone wall. Brilliant spotlights were attached at regular intervals along the top of the wall, aligned toward the field. A half-dozen towering structures reared skyward on the far side of the wall.

Sundance uttered a low whistle.

Blade glanced to the right.

Two soldiers were strolling along the base of the wall, AK-47's slung over their shoulders, coming toward the Warriors.

Blade ducked from sight. Gaining entrance to the Ministry promised to be extremely difficult. Crossing the field unseen, if guards were posted on the wall, would be impossible. And sneaking in the front gate was a ludicrous notion.

Or was it?

Blade waited until the two guards passed and were 50 yards off, nearing the gate. He waved to Sundance, then followed the guards, staying behind the trees.

The guards ambled at a leisurely pace.

Sundance caught up with Blade. "What are you doing?" he whispered.

"There's no way we'll get over that wall," Blade responded. "Not with all the lights and the barbed wire and the guards."

"So how do we get inside?"

"I'm working on that," Blade informed him.

The pair of patrolling guards reached the gate and halted, engaging the quartet of soldiers already there in conversation.

Blade edged to within 20 yards of the front gate, then squatted in the shelter of a large oak.

Sundance joined the head Warrior.

The light on the eastern horizon was increasing.

Blade scrutinized the wall, at a loss for an idea to penetrate the Ministry's defenses.

A muted rumble sounded from the northwest.

Blade glanced over his left shoulder.

A truck was slowly approaching the gate, still about 400 yards distant.

Blade squinted, striving to identify the truck. He wasn't worried about being observed by the truck's occupants; the trees were plunged in murky shadows.

The truck drove nearer.

Blade perceived the truck wasn't a military vehicle. It was white, with a small cab and a square body.

The truck was 350 yards off.

Blade glanced at the gate, then the truck.

The truck reached the 300-yard mark.

Blade turned to Sundance. "I don't have time to explain. I want you to stay here, right here, until I signal you or return."

"What? Where are you going?" Sundance asked.

"No time," Blade stated, and rose. He ran to the rear, keeping in the darkest areas, racing parallel with the road. His plan was perilous, but if he succeeded, he would be inside the Ministry in a matter of minutes. But he had to reach the 100-yard mark before the white truck.

The truck was 250 yards from the gate.

Blade sprinted full out, his eyes glued to the inky section of road next to an enormous willow tree. If he could reach that spot before the truck, and if his estimation of the truck's size was accurate, he could carry it off.

If.

The white truck was now 200 yards from the front gate.

Blade almost stumbled over a root. He recovered and sped toward the willow.

One hundred eighty yards.

Blade wished there had been time to detail his intent to Sundance. He knew Sundance would chafe at being left behind, but both of them trying for the truck was unrealistic, increasing their risk of detection. And as the tallest, Blade stood the best chance of accomplishing the maneuver.

One hundred sixty yards.

Damn! His legs ached! Blade ignored the pain, pounding forward, breathing deeply.

One hundred fifty yards.

If he tripped again, he was lost.

One hundred forty.

Blade slowed, slinging the Commando over his right shoulder.

One hundred thirty.

Blade reached the cover of the willow and pressed against its rough trunk, the bark scraping his right cheek.

One hundred twenty.

He would only get one try. If he blew it, they could forget locating the Vikings in the Ministry. If the Vikings were even there.

If again.

One hundred ten.

Blade tensed, watching the tires turn as the white truck neared the willow tree. He estimated the truck was moving at 30 miles an hour.

The white truck reached the spreading willow, was abreast of the trunk for an instant, and then was past the willow, proceeding toward the gate.

Blade was in motion as the truck came even with the willow. He darted around the trunk and dashed the five feet to the road, reaching the rear corner, his legs churning to keep pace, his arms outstretched, his fingers grasping for a purchase. For a second, the outcome was in doubt. And then his fingers closed on the corner, his nails gaining a slight hold on the metal, but it was enough for him to exert his tremendous strength, to tug on the corner, to pull his body that much closer to the rear panel of the vehicle, and there was a door handle in the center of the white panel. His left arm swung out, and he grabbed the handle and held on for dear life. The strain was incredible. His feet left the road, and for a moment he was hanging by one hand as his right was wrenched from the corner. He clawed at the handle with his right hand, gripping the cool metal, and used his added leverage to haul himself onto the rear fender.

The truck was 80 yards from the iron gate.

Blade glanced up. The roof was eight feet above his head. He steeled his leg muscles and leaped, his arms straight overhead, and his hands clasped the lip of the roof as his knees banged against the rear panel. He grimaced as he clung to the roof, knowing he must keep moving or he would falter and fall to the asphalt. His arms bulged, his neck muscles protruding, as he pulled himself up onto the roof.

Fifty yards from the dull horizontal and vertical iron bars.

Blade rolled to the middle of the roof. Two of his fingers were bleeding and his left knee was throbbing. But he'd done it!

The small white truck was reducing its speed. There was a slight squeaking noise from the cab, from the driver's side, as if the driver was rolling his window down.

Only four guards were at the gate. The two on patrol, Blade reasoned, must have resumed their rounds.

The truck came to a halt in front of the gate.

"Hi, Tim," said one of the guards. "You're late."

"I had to wait for them to get their asses in gear at my last stop," the driver, evidently the man named Tim, stated. "They couldn't find a bag of dirty aprons from last night."

"There's a note attached to my clipboard," the guard said. "They want you to pick up a load from Penza Hall."

"All right," the driver responded. "But I hope they have it all on the loading dock. I hate going into that place. It gives me the creeps."

"Just be thankful you're not in there as a permanent resident," the guard remarked, grinning.

"Don't even joke about a thing like that," Tim said. "I'm not an enemy of the State."

The guard snickered. He motioned toward the gate. "Open it!" he ordered.

The three other guards obeyed.

Blade, lying as flat as possible on the roof, felt the truck vibrate as it passed the iron gate. He'd made it! He was inside the Ministry of Psychological Sciences!

Now what?

The white truck took a right, along a narrow, tree-lined road. Few people were abroad.

Blade could hear the driver whistling as he drove. What was this Tim picking up at Penza Hall? And why was the driver so leery of the place? What was it Tim had said to the guard? "I'm not an enemy of the State."

Was Penza Hall a prison? Hardly likely, if the complex was devoted to the Psychological Sciences. Unless, Blade speculated, Penza Hall was devoted to psychological manipulations instead of simple physical incarceration. He recalled a portion of his Warrior course at the Home, a study of the psychological-warfare techniques employed by the superpowers and others before the Big Blast. The Russians, in particular, masters of mind manipulation, and at extracting important data from recalcitrant subjects. Perhaps Penza Hall was where such "extractions" were made. If so, then Penza Hall might be where the Vikings were being interrogated.

The truck took a left, driving between two high buildings, each over ten stories in height.

Blade peered up at the windows, hoping no one was gazing through them at the road below.

The white truck turned to the right, slowing.

Blade rose on his elbows and scanned the road ahead. They were entering an expansive parking lot. Across the lot was a gigantic structure, only four stories high but encompassing at least five or six acres. Most of the windows in the edifice were dark; only three or four displayed any light. The truck was making for a loading dock stacked with crates and boxes. Two enormous doors, both closed, each large enough to accommodate a troop transport or a tractor-trailer, framed the wall behind the loading dock.

The driver ceased whistling.

Blade lowered his head, waiting with baited breath as the truck braked alongside the loading dock. He heard a door slam and risked a look.

The driver, a lean individual in jeans and a blue jacket, was ascending the ramp to the loading dock, a tablet in his left hand. He walked to the right of the two immense doors, up to a small metal door. He reached up and pressed a button encased in the brown wall.

Blade detected a faint ringing from within the building. He gazed at the structure, attempting to determine the material used in its construction. The brown wall appeared to be a form of stone, but he doubted stone was the material used. Was it a plastic designed to simulate the appearance of stone? Or was it a substance the Soviets had developed since the Big Blast?

The small door suddenly opened, and a brawny soldier stood in the doorway. "Yes?" he demanded.

The driver pointed toward his truck. "They told me at the gate you have a pickup."

The guard glanced at the white truck. "Sure do. Wait right here." He started to turn, then paused. "On second thought, why don't you come with me?"

Tim fidgeted nervously. "Do I have to?"

The guard grinned. "Afraid so. There's about eight or nine bins. I'm not going to lug it all down here by myself."

Tim shrugged. "Then let's hop to it."

The guard and the driver disappeared inside.

Blade saw his chance. He rolled to the right and dropped from the roof, alighting on his hands and feet, his arches stinging from the impact.

No one else was in sight.

Blade stood and headed for the ramp. As he did, he noticed the sign on the side panel of the white truck: CENTRAL LAUNDRY. A laundry truck? The Ministry sent its soiled garments and whatever to another establishment to be cleaned? Why not clean them on the premises? Perhaps because doing so would entail a permanent cleaning staff at the Ministry, and such a staff would present a security problem. What was the old saying? Loose lips sink ships? Considering the security clamped on the Ministry, the higher-ups undoubtedly wanted to minimize the presence of non-essential personnel. He reached the ramp and raced up to the loading dock.

A crack of light rimmed the small door.

Blade jogged to the door and halted, unslinging the Commando. The door was slightly ajar! When the guard and driver had entered Penza Hall, they had failed to push the door closed! Maybe because they would be returning with their arms laden with laundry. He used his left hand to ease the door open.

A gloomy, deserted hallway was on the other side.

Blade ducked through the door and flattened against the left-hand wall.

The hallway ended at a yellow door 20 yards away. Other doors lined the hallway, four on the left, three on the right.

There was no time to lose! The guard and the driver might return at any moment!

Blade reached the first door on the left. It was open, revealing a spacious chamber filled with stacks of wooden crates and cardboard boxes.

The yellow door at the end of the hall started to swing open.

Blade slid into the storage chamber and hid behind a stack of crates as the hallway filled with a peculiar squeaking.

" . . . three more loads," said the voice of the guard.

"Thanks for doing this," stated the driver. "Rostov always makes me go up and get it by myself."

"Rostov is a prick," the guard stated.

Blade heard the metal door open, and he padded to the doorway and risked a peek around the corner.

The guard and the driver were pushing white bins overflowing with unclean clothing and linen. The squeaking was emanating from the tiny black wheels on the laundry bins. They passed outside, and the metal door eased almost shut.

Blade turned to the left and sprinted down the hallway to the yellow door. The door opened onto a flight of stairs. He hesitated, glancing down. The stairs descended several levels below ground, as well as climbing to the stories above. Which way to go? The guard and the driver would be going up. So he went down, taking two steps at a stride, constantly surveying the levels below for any hint of activity. He halted on the first landing, pondering. If the Russians did hold the Vikings in Penza Hall, on which floor would the Vikings most likely be detained? Surely not on one of the upper floors, where windows were a tempting escape route.

Underground would be best.

Move! his mind shrieked.

Blade hastened below. It was close to dawn, and the corridors would probably be crammed with workers once the day shift arrived. Finding the holding cells quickly was imperative. He decided to begin at the bottom and work his way up. The magnitude of his task bothered him. Penza Hall was enormous. He couldn't possibly cover all of it before daylight. He reached the next landing, kept moving.

Far above him a door scraped open.

Someone else was using the stairs!

Blade increased his pace. Three steps at a leap, he hurried to the lowest level.

Footsteps sounded on the stairs above, echoing hollowly in the confines of the stairwell.

Blade reached the bottom of the stairwell and found two yellow doors. He tried one knob, and was gratified when it twisted and the door jerked wide. Gratified until he saw what awaited him.

A Russian soldier.

15

Sundance was annoyed. He resented being left behind, but he was too professional a Warrior to disobey his orders. So he waited, concealed in the weeds near the large oak, watching the four guards at the gate. He had covered them with the FN 50-63 when the white truck had stopped, but the guards hadn't seen Blade. His respect for the Warrior chief had ballooned; only an idiot or a dedicated, courageous man would have attempted such a perilous strategem. The idiot because he wouldn't know any better. The brave man because the mission was of paramount importance, and the danger was eclipsed by an exalted ideal, the ideal of serving others, of saving lives, of placing a priority on the welfare of the many and rendering any sacrifice necessary. And Blade wasn't an idiot.

The eastern sky was growing lighter and lighter.

Sundance had caught a glimpse of Blade's maneuver, and had marveled at the speed, strength, and daring displayed. He knew Blade viewed this run to Philadelphia as critical to the Family's future. If an alliance could be forged with the Vikings, the Soviets would be defeated that much sooner. If the Vikings weren't receptive to the idea, the Family faced the prospect of a prolonged conflict with the Russians. By finding the Vikings and liberating them, Blade might save untold millions from the totalitarian Communist regime, might restore sweet liberty to the land.

There was a commotion to the right.

Sundance craned his neck to see better.

Two more guards were approaching the front gate, patrolling along the base of the wall. They had stopped, and were staring at the line of trees, AK-47's in hand.

Someone was shouting.

The two guards began walking across the field toward the trees.

What was happening? Sundance wondered.

He found out.

Captain Georgii Bakunin emerged from the woods, yelling in Russian, hurrying up to the two soldiers. They conversed for a few seconds, and Bakunin showed them something he drew from his pocket.

The four gate guards were watching the trio.

Sundance crawled to the base of the oak and stood, carefully avoiding exposing himself to the soldiers. He peered around the trunk.

Bakunin and the pair of guards were jogging toward the front gate.

Sundance stared at Bakunin, knowing the captain would alert the Ministry to the presence of the Warriors. They would conduct an extensive search of the grounds and the building, and they would increase their perimeter security, minimizing Blade's chances of eascaping. The Warrior chief would be trapped inside.

Bakunin and the two guards were 50 yards from the

gate.

What should he do? Sundance doubted Bakunin had told the two troopers about Blade and himself. They'd only exchanged a few words. Bakunin must have told them who he was, and produced confirming identification.

Bakunin and the two soldiers were 40 yards from the iron gate.

Sundance placed his finger on the trigger of the FN. If Bakunin was silenced before he could inform the Ministry officials, the Russians would never suspect Blade was inside. Particularly if a diversion was created *outside.*

Bakunin and the two guards were running along the base of the wall.

Sundance raised the FN to his shoulder. If he downed Bakunin, all hell would break loose! The Russians would come pouring out of the Ministry after him. But if he could hold them off for a while, he might give Blade the precious time necessary to locate the Vikings. He sighted on Bakunin, aiming for the head.

Bakunin and the two patrol guards were 20 yards from the front gate, in a direct line with a large oak at the edge of the field, when the captain's head exploded in a spray of blood and brains, spattering the wall, and he was lifted from his feet and smashed against the stone as the sound of a shot shattered the dawn air.

The two guards with Bakunin spun toward the tree line, and both were rocked backward as powerful slugs ripped through their torsos and flung them to the ground, spurting crimson from their ruptured chests.

Initially stunned by the carnage, the quartet of gate guards sprang into action. Three of them spread out, eyes riveted on the woods, seeking the sniper. The fourth ran toward a black button imbedded in the wall to the left of the gate. He was reaching for the button when a slug caught him in the back of the head, just above the neck, and his mouth and nose erupted outward in a shower of flesh and teeth. He tumbled onto his stomach and lay still.

The three remaining soldiers hesitated. One of them

turned and dashed for the gate, intending to open it and seek shelter inside. But three shots struck him in the middle of his back, between his shoulder blades, and he was hurled forward to crash into the unyielding iron gate. He slumped to the earth.

One of the guards spotted a faint gun flash near the large oak, and charged, firing his AK-47 at the tree, his rounds chipping bark from the trunk. He managed four strides before he was hit in the right eye. His body jerked to the right and flopped to the grass.

The last guard, having seen his comrades die and realizing there was nowhere he could flee, dropped his AK-47 and raised his hands above his head, mustering a feeble grin. His grin vanished, collapsing inward and filling his mouth with blood and chunks of teeth, as a shot penetrated his mouth and exited out the back of his neck. A look of amazement flitted across his features, and he tottered and fell.

Sundance raced from cover, sprinting the 20 yards to the wall and then running to the gate. He stepped over the body of one of the guards, peering inside.

Lights were coming on in a low structure approximately 50 yards distant, to the left of the front gate.

Sundance leaned against the wall and hastily replaced the partially spent magazine in the FN. He wanted a full clip when the soldiers arrived on the scene. He tossed the partially spent magazine aside and pulled a fresh clip from his right rear pants pocket. As he inserted the magazine, loud shouting arose from within the complex. He glanced around the corner of the wall, between the iron gate bars.

A cluster of 10 to 12 troopers had gathered at the entrance to the low structure. They were yelling and gesturing toward the front gate.

Sundance grinned. He suspected the low structure was a barracks for the soldiers. They would need to cross a wide lawn before reaching the gate, and would be sitting ducks for 40 yards or so. A row of trees lined the road beyond the gate, but the road and the trees would be to the right. A long drive connected the barracks to the road, and someone had thoughtfully neglected to line the drive with trees.

More shouting. Seven of the Russian soldiers started running in the direction of the gate.

Sundance rested the FN barrel on one of the horizontal bars in the iron gate. He patiently waited until the soldiers were only 30 yards off, then squeezed the trigger and held it down.

The seven troopers jerked and thrashed as they were hit. Only one of them was able to get off a shot. Surprised in the open, they died en masse, their bodies bunched together.

Louder yelling from the barracks.

Sundance took a deep breath to calm himself. His blood was racing, his adrenaline pumping. In a strange sort of way, he was enjoying himself, despite the overwhelming odds. He'd fought in the battle for the Home against the Doktor's forces, but this was different, different even than fighting the scavengers. This time it was him against an army, and he relished the challenge. He would buy Blade the time the Warrior chief needed, or he would perish in the attempt.

Soldiers continued to pile from the barracks. An officer took command, and with a wave of his right arm led ten of them toward the gate.

Sundance sighted the FN.

It was do-or-die time!

16

The Russian soldier, a private, was carrying a tray of dirty dishes and an empty carton of milk. He inadvertently started as a giant wrenched the door in front of him open, but then he saw the uniform and grinned. "Comrade! You scared the hell out of me!"

Blade froze. The soldier had an AK-47 slung over his left shoulder.

The young guard glanced over his shoulder at the gloomy hallway, then stared at Blade, his expression evidencing a certain nervousness. "You won't report me, will you?"

"Report you?" Blade repeated.

The soldier hefted the tray. "I know we are not permitted to eat on duty, but I become so bored at night when there is little to do, and my friend in the kitchen . . ." He abruptly stopped, his eyes narrowing, focused on the Commando.

Blade bent his right leg at the knee.

"Where did you get that weapon?" the guard asked. "That is not standard issue." He raked Blade from head to toe. "And your uniform does not seem quite right," he stupidly blurted out.

Blade flicked his right leg out, striking the guard on the left kneecap. There was a distinct snapping noise, and the guard gasped and dropped his food tray. Blade's left hand gripped the guard by the shirt before he could fall. The tray clattered to the tiled floor. Blade moved into the hallway, closing the door behind him. He shoved the Commando barrel into the guard's frightened face.

"Please!" the guard cried. "Don't kill me!"

"That depends on you!" Blade informed him.

The guard's thin lips were quivering. "I think my knee is broken!"

"You knee will be the least of your problems if you don't cooperate," Blade stated menacingly.

"What do you want?" the guard wailed.

"The Vikings."

The guard's brown eyes widened. "The Vikings?"

"Are you hard of hearing?" Blade snapped. "Where are they?" He decided to try a bluff. "And don't play games with me! I know they're here!"

"They were here," the guard exclaimed.

"What do you mean?"

The guard motioned toward a series of doors in the hallway to their rear. "They were held here while the Committee for State Security questioned them."

"And what happened to them?" Blade queried.

The guard's mouth turned downward. "They . . . did not survive the questioning."

"They died?" Blade probed.

The guard nodded.

Blade jammed the Commando barrel into the guard's cheek. "I don't believe you!"

"It's true!" the guard insisted in terror. "The last one died four days ago! The Security people were not lenient in their interrogations!"

Blade frowned. He'd anticipated this eventuality, but dreaded it all the same. Too much time had elapsed since the Vikings were captured, and the Soviets were not notorious for allowing their captives to live once the required information had been obtained.

The information!

"Where's their office?" Blade demanded.

"What?" the guard responded, perplexed.

"The office of the Committee for State Security," Blade said.

The guard blanched. "You are joking, yes?"

Blade's countenance hardened. "Do I look like I'm joking?"

"But it would be im—" the guard started to object.

Blade smacked the Commando barrel against the guard's head. "They must have an office in this building! Somewhere where they could conduct their interrogations in private! Where is it?"

The guard pressed his left hand to his injured ear. "Upstairs," he answered.

"How far up?" Blade asked.

"Three floors," the guard revealed.

"Come on!" Blade yanked the guard toward the door.

"What are you doing?"

"You're going to take me to their office," Blade told him.

"No!" the guard protested. "They will kill me when they find out!"

Blade paused. "I won't tell them if you don't! But I

will kill you right here and now if you don't take me to their office! So what's it going to be?"

The guard was clearly scared out of his wits.

Blade shoved him toward the door. "Get going!"

Whining, the guard hobbled to the door and opened it.

"Up the stairwell!" Blade barked. "Move it!"

They ascended the stairs, proceeding slowly, impeded by the guard's injured knee. As they reached the appropriate landing, a muted siren began wailing in the distance.

Blade halted. "What's that?"

The guard cocked his head. "The security alarm."

Blade rammed the Commando barrel into the guard's back. "They must know I'm here!"

"I don't think so!" the guard replied, afraid of receiving a round in the spinal column.

"Why?"

"It sounds like it is coming from out near the barracks," the guard explained, hoping to alleviate the giant's obvious tension and reduce his risk of being shot. "If they knew you were here, the alarms in Penza Hall would go off."

Blade gazed up the stairwell. Why would they be blaring an alarm outside? Did it have something to do with Sundance? "Keep moving!" he ordered.

The guard cautiously eased open one of the two yellow doors, the one on the left, and looked in both directions. "All clear," he claimed.

Blade pushed the guard into the hallway, then followed. The corridor was indeed deserted. "Where's their office?"

"This way," the guard said, pointing to the right.

Blade nudged the guard with the Commando. "Lead the way."

The guard limped down the hall and stopped at one of the many doors. "This is it."

Blade glanced at the door. Printed in English—along with strange letters from another language, undoubtedly Russian—were the words. COMMITTEE

FOR STATE SECURITY. STAFF PERSONNEL ONLY. "Try the knob," Blade directed.

The guard did. "It is locked."

"Step aside." Blade waited while the guard shuffled a few feet further along the corridor. He placed his right hand on the door and tested the knob, verifying the door was locked.

"See? We can't get in," the guard said. "We should leave!"

Blade's right arm tightened, his massive muscles rippling, as he applied his prodigious strength to the lock. He grit his teeth, concentrating on the door, and he almost missed the guard's attack. A glimmer of flashing light alerted him at the last instant.

The guard had drawn a knife from concealment, and he made a growling noise deep in his throat as he stabbed the sharp knife up and in, going for the giant's chest. He believed he'd caught the giant completely unawares, so he was all the more surprised when his first blow missed, and was amazed when the giant swung the machine-gun barrel toward him but didn't squeeze the trigger. The guard realized the giant wouldn't shoot because the shots would bring troops on the run. He waved the knife in the air. "I'm going to carve you up into little pieces for what you did to my knee!" he stated confidently. He failed to notice the giant's right hand as it inched under his bulky uniform shirt.

"You talk too much," the giant said.

"Do I?" the guard rejoined, and slashed his knife at the giant's face.

Blade easily evaded the knife, drawing his face out of range, and then stepped in close and swept the right Bowie out and up, the 15-inch blade burying itself to the hilt in the stupefied guard's throat below the chin.

The guard stiffened and dropped his knife, gurgling as his blood poured from his neck. He gasped and futilely endeavored to withdraw the Bowie, but the giant's steely arm held the blade fast. He opened his mouth to speak, but only a rivulet of blood ushered forth. His eyelids fluttered, and he expired.

Blade wrenched the Bowie free, his hand and forearm caked with dripping crimson.

The guard pitched to the floor.

Blade wiped the Bowie clean on the guard's pant leg, then slid the big knife into its sheath. He quickly slung the Commando over his right shoulder, then applied both of his hands to the doorknob. Straining his arms to the utmost, he simultaneously pushed and twisted. For half a minute nothing transpired. And then the inner jamb rent with a splintering crunch, and the door swung open, the doorknob snapping off in his hands.

The siren was still wailing in the distance.

Blade entered the KGB office. There were doors to his left and right. Against the right wall was a desk; against the left wall a file cabinet. He moved to the cabinet and tried the top drawer.

The damn thing was locked.

Blade returned to the hallway and found the guard's knife. It had a relatively thick six-inch blade. He re-entered the office, crossed to the file cabinet, and gripped the top drawer with his right hand while holding the knife, blade pointed downward, in his left. He exerted pressure on the drawer, and was rewarded by a quarter inch gap appearing at the top of the drawer. He inserted the knife blade all the way to the handle, and started prying on the drawer with the knife while pulling on the handle with his right hand. A minute elapsed. Two. The drawer came open with a resounding metallic pop. He paused and listened.

The corridor was quiet.

Blade rummaged through the dozens of folders in the top drawer. They were all labeled, some in Russian, some in English. None of them appeared to have any connection with the Vikings. He leaned over and tugged on the second drawer, delighted when it slid right open. A hasty search was fruitless. He knelt and opened the third, final, drawer.

And there they were.

Three manilla files, each headed with the word VIKINGS. He scooped them out and flipped through the pages. Some of the contents were in Russian, some in English. He wondered why. He knew the Russians were bilingual. They had to be. Many of their troopers were conscripted, brainwashed Americans. Many of the bureaucrats were native citizens as well, and perhaps the conquered Americans found it too difficult to learn Russian fluently. Perhaps the reports in the files were duplicated, one in Russian, one in English. Whatever the case, Blade determined, now was not the time to reflect on the issue. He extracted the files, unbuttoned his shirt, and tucked them over his abdomen. Hurriedly buttoning the shirt, he rose and started for the door.

That was when the brainstorm hit.

Blade halted, went to the desk, and tried several of its drawers. None of them were locked. He discovered a fingernail file, a brush, a mirror in the second one he opened. In the third he found a pack of matches. Smiling, he walked to the KGB files and opened all three drawers. He lit a match, then touched the flame to the files. A folder sparked, then burst into flame. He swiftly repeated the procedure with each drawer. The room was filled with smoke by the time he stood, dropped the matches into the top drawer, and ran into the corridor.

The KGB was in for a nasty surprise.

Blade jogged toward the stairwell. He had the information the Freedom Federation needed. But it wouldn't be of any use if he didn't make it out of the Ministry alive. He flung the stairwell door open, stepped onto the landing.

"Freeze!" someone bellowed from overhead.

Blade glanced up.

A Russian soldier was leaning over the railing half a flight above, his AK-47 trained on the Warrior.

17

"Where do you think your friends went?" Libby asked.

"I don't know," Bertha admitted.

"Maybe they split on you," pudgy Eddy suggested.

"And left the SEAL here?" Bertha rejoined.

They were standing next to the transport. The sun was just cresting the eastern horizon. None of the Claws had been able to sleep after the incident with the nocturnal Hunter. Shortly before daybreak, Cole had recommended finding Bertha's friends. Libby and Eddy came along. The rest were told to remain in the cabin.

"They'll be back," Cole said.

"If they don't get racked," Eddy commented.

Bertha glanced at Pudgy. "Boy! Ain't you the cheery one!"

"What the hell do I have to be happy about?" Eddy responded.

"How about getting out of there, for one thing," Libby remarked.

"I'll believe it when I see it," was Eddy's retort.

Bertha leaned against the SEAL. The doors were locked, and only Blade had a key. There was nothing she could do, nowhere she could go, until Blade and Sundance returned. But who knew how long that could take? They must have departed for Philadelphia last night! She was slightly miffed they had gone on without her. But she knew the Big Guy pretty well, knew he wouldn't allow anything to interfere with the mission. Usually. There had been that time in Thief River Falls.

"So what do we do now?" Libby inquired. She, like Cole and Eddy, carried an AK-47.

"We wait for my buddies," Bertha stated.

"How long? A day? A week?" Eddy asked.

Cole glared at Eddy. "Shut up," he snapped.

Eddy did.

Bertha studied Cole. The Claw leader had been

abnormally silent on the trek from the log cabin. What was he thinking about? The prospect of living at the home? Of delivering the Claws from a savage existence of survival of the fittest?

"We could leave one of us here," Libby proposed, "and the rest of us could wait at the cabin." She paused. "I don't like leaving the younger ones alone."

"They can take care of themselves," Eddy said.

Cole stared in the general direction of their hideout. "Libby, you can stay here with Bertha. Eddy and I will go back."

"Fine by me," Libby stated.

"Hey!" Eddy said. "Do you guys hear something?"

Bertha suddenly did, and an icy sensation crept over her skin. Gunshots. Coming from the . . .

"The cabin!" Cole shouted, and was off, racing at breakneck speed.

Libby and Eddy took off after him.

Bertha clutched her M-16 and followed. The three Claws were able to traverse the terrain at an uncanny speed. Years of practice had endowed them with exceptionally fleet feet and remarkable skill at negotiating obstacles in their path. She was able to keep Libby and Eddy in sight, but couldn't gain on them. Her forehead began hurting again. She'd examined the wound during the night. There was a ragged two-inch gash along her hairline, but otherwise she seemed to be fine. She doubted she had a concussion. Her head had sustained tremendous blows in the past. Hickok liked to say it was the hardest head he knew of. But what did he know?

The distant gunfire attained a crescendo. Screams and shrieks were distinguishable.

Bertha abruptly forget all else in her concern for the Claws. She hadn't considered them to be in any grave danger until that very instant. After all, those kids had spent years surviving in the wilderness of Valley Forge, fighting Hunters and other Packrats, stealing food and guns and whatever else they required. She knew there existed a violent rivalry among the Packrat gangs for control of the large but limited tract of land comprising Valley Forge. But the Packrats were, for the most part, young children, and she'd never seriously considered them as being decidedly deadly.

She was about to have her impression changed.

Bertha was still hundreds of yards from the log cabin when the shooting died down. A ghastly screech reached her ears, then all was unnaturally quiet. She ran a little faster. Eddy and Libby were about 20 yards ahead of her. They reached the field at the bottom of the burned-out hill and started across. Bertha was breathing heavily, and her left side began hurting as she neared the base of the hill. Ignoring the pain in her side, she took a deep breath and plunged forward across the field.

Cole was nowhere in sight, but Libby and Eddy were 30 yards in front of her.

Bertha poured on the steam, and was again only 20 yards behind the duo when they entered the trees.

Someone screamed.

Bertha clutched her M-16 in both hands and jogged into the woods. She darted through the brush and among the trees until she spied the clearing and the cabin, and then she halted, stunned.

The log cabin resembled a sieve. The door had been shot to pieces, riddled with bullets until whole sections had fallen off. The windows had fared worse; all of the glass panes were gone, and the edges where chipped and pockmarked. Even the cabin walls had been perforated again and again and again by heavy-caliber slugs. Bodies were everywhere. Bodies of the Claws. Most of them were congregated near the door, as if they'd been gunned down in the act of fleeing the cabin. A few had tumbled into the pit. Blood soaked the ground.

"Lordy!" Bertha exclaimed, walking up to the clearing.

Cole was on his knees to the left of the cabin door. The body of the young girl, Milly, was cradled in his lap. Her forehead had been blown off. Tears streaked his cheeks as he rocked back and forth. His lips were trembling. "No!" he cried. "No! No! No!"

Libby and Eddy stood near the pit. Libby appeared to be in a state of shock. Eddy, by contrast, was livid, his pudgy features contorted in rage.

"They're . . . all . . . dead!" Libby stated in a dazed, surveying the massacre.

"How?" Eddy demanded. "Where were the guards? We posted guards before we left!"

"Maybe," Libby said, her eyes watering, "maybe the guards were killed before they could sound the alarm."

Eddy pointed at the log cabin. "And what the hell did that? Those walls were thick! They could stand up to an AK-47! That's why we picked this place. But look at them! Look at the size of those holes!"

"Who cares about the holes?" Libby asked, sniffling.

"I do!" Eddy rejoined. "I want to know what the hell I'm going up against when I catch up with whoever did this!"

"What?" Libby said, glancing at Eddy.

"You heard me!" Eddy declared. "They can't have gotten far! I'm going after them right now!"

Libby grabbed Eddy's left arm. "No! You can't!"

"And why the hell can't I?" Eddy retorted.

"You won't stand a chance," Libby protested.

Eddy motioned toward the corpses. "And what chance did they have, Libby? Look at them! Some of them weren't even armed! We can't let the bastards who did this get away!"

"No," Libby objected. "That isn't the way."

"Yes, it is!" Cole thundered, rising to his feet, his face an iron mask. "Eddy's right! We're going to waste the sons of bitches responsible for this!"

Libby took a few steps toward Cole. "But, Cole . . ."

"There's no buts about it!" Cole cut her off. "We're going to avenge them!" He pointed at Milly's pathetic body. "This was our fault, Libby! We owe it to them!"

"Our fault?" Libby repeated. "How was it our fault? We've left the younger ones alone before. Burt was with them, and he was twelve. He knew the score. All of them did! So how do you figure this was our fault? We weren't even here!"

"We should have been," Cole said softly.

"But we weren't," Libby persisted.

Cole pressed his right hand on his forehead and

looked around. "We were all so damn excited about getting out of here! About finding a place where we could live free! And we forgot where we were! We forgot what could happen if we dropped our guard."

"But you did everything you could have done!" Libby said. "You can't blame yourself!"

Cole wiped his hand across his eyes. When he stared at Libby, his gaze was flinty. "Can't I?" He paused, sighed wearily, then inspected his AK-47. "Eddy and I are going after the bastards. Are you coming?"

"We don't have to do this!" Libby pleaded. "We can still leave with Bertha and her friends!"

Cole glanced at Bertha. "This isn't your fight. You don't have to come."

"There's nothin' I can do to talk you out of goin'?" Bertha asked.

Cole shook his head. "Don't even try. You'd be wasting your breath!"

Tears were flowing down Libby's face. "Cole! Please! You know what will happen!"

Cole gazed into Libby's eyes. "I know."

Bertha didn't know what to say. She knew Cole was determined to get his revenge. What could she do to stop him, short of shooting him herself? She admired him, even felt a peculiar kinship to Cole. Maybe, she speculated, it had something to do with her gang days in the Twin Cities. Oh, her life had been different in several ways. Cole and many of the other Packrats had come from good homes where they usually had enough food and even enjoyed some luxuries. Luxuries like decent clothes, and shoes, and even schooling. The Packrats had lost it all when their parents had been executed or imprisoned by the Communists. Bertha and her companions in the Twin Cities had never had it so good, never enjoyed even the basic necessities on a regular basis, never known what it was like to have a stable home environment in their early years. But in others respects, her former gang and the Packrats had a lot in common. There were always enemies out to get them, and no one outside the gang could be trusted.

You survived if you were quick and alert. You died if you slipped for an instant. Under such harsh conditions, strong bonds were forged. Deep friendships. And in Cole's case, the affection was compounded by the fact many of the Packrats were so young, so vulnerable, and had relied on his judgment. Bertha saw the anguish on his face, and recognized she couldn't begin to appreciate the depth of the torment he must be feeling.

Libby turned to Bertha. "Please! Don't let them go!"

Bertha frowned. "There's nothin' I can do."

Libby uttered a whining noise and covered her eyes with her left hand.

Eddy was checking his AK-47.

"Eddy," Cole said.

"Yeah?" Eddy responded.

"Find their trail," Cole directed, and entered the cabin.

Eddy smiled. "You got it." He began searching the ground near the edge of the woods.

Bertha moved over to Libby and draped her right arm across the girl's shoulders.

"I don't want him to go," Libby mumbled. "He'll be killed!"

"Maybe not," Bertha said.

Libby looked up, her eyes red, her cheeks moist. "Yes, he will! I just know it!"

"You love him, don't you?" Bertha asked gently.

Libby sniffed and nodded, glancing at the cabin.

"Does he love you?" Bertha inquired.

"I don't know," Libby admitted. "I think so. I feel he does, in my heart. But he's never shown it. Never come right out and said he does. I don't know why. Maybe he's afraid. Afraid of losing me like he did his mom and dad. You don't have any idea what it's like to love someone, and not have them love you!"

Want to bet? Bertha almost said. Instead, she held her peace, contemplating her own relationship with the Family's superlative gunfighter, Hickok. But could she justify calling it a relationship? She'd pined after that dummy for what seemed like ages! And where had it gotten her? True, Hickok had been the first man she'd ever fallen for, head-over-heels in love. True, he was the choicest specimen of manhood she'd ever seen. Hunk de la hunk, so to speak. How long, though, could she justify yearning for a man unable to reciprocate her devotion? Hickok was married to Sherry, and Bertha knew the gunman well enough to know he would remain loyal to Sherry while Sherry lived, and maybe even afterwards. The Family ardently believed life did not end with death. The Elders taught that death was merely the technique of ascending from the material level to a higher, more spiritual plane. Even if Sherry passed on, Hickok was just the type to stay loyal to her, firmly expecting he would see her again after his own earthly demise. So what the hell am I doing, Bertha asked herself, wasting my time with someone I'll never have a chance with? She studied the miserable Libby, and finally acknowledged how very lonely she'd been while yearning for Hickok. Maybe it was about time she faced facts; sometimes, love was one-sided; sometimes, a person could deeply love another, and the feeling wouldn't be mutual.

Cole emerged from the log cabin, his features set in grim lines. "All the ones left inside are dead," he remarked. "Whoever did this took all of our weapons."

"Whoever did this is heading to the south," Eddy announced, joining them.

Cole stared at Eddy. "The Bobcats?"

"I think so," Eddy confirmed.

"Let's do it," Cole said, and started to the south.

Libby dabbed at her eyes with her fingers. "Wait for me!"

Cole stopped and turned. "You stay here with Bertha."

"I'm coming," Libby declared.

"I'd feel better if you didn't," Cole said. "Go back to Bertha's buggy and wait for her friends."

"I'm coming," Libby reiterated.

"Let her come, Cole," Eddy chimed in.

Cole frowned. "All right. But stay close to me! I

don't want anything to happen to you."

"You don't?" Libby responded, brightening.

"Let's go!" Cole directed. He wheeled and stalked into the woods, followed by Eddy.

Libby took off after them. "I hope I see you again, soon," she stated to Bertha over her right shoulder.

Bertha hesitated. This wasn't her fight. Cole was right. But she was, in a sense, partially to blame for the slaughter. Her presence, and her promise of salvation for the Claws, had distracted them, had diverted Cole from his responsibilities as Claw leader. She looked at little Milly. That child's death was on her shoulders, whether she liked it or not.

Libby vanished in the trees.

Maybe she owed it to them to help. Maybe she owed it to them to keep Cole, Libby, and Eddy alive, so they could savor the freedom the others had dreamed about. And maybe she owed it to herself, because they were her newfound friends, and once she was attached to someone, she never abandoned them. Hickok was a case in point.

"Oh, hell!" Bertha exclaimed. She jogged toward the forest. "Wait up!" she called.

Libby, ten yards into the woods, stopped. "What are you doing?" she inquired as Bertha ran up.

Bertha could see Cole and Eddy, waiting for them 30 yards off. "I'm comin' with you."

"Go back!" Libby urged. "We can do this alone!"

Bertha shook her head. "No one," she said emphatically, "should ever have to be alone." She paused for emphasis. "Not ever! Now let's teach these Bobcats a lesson they'll never forget!"

18

What was keeping Blade?

Sundance sighted on the officer and the ten troopers, and waited until they were in the middle of the lawn before he fired. The officer pitched to the ground, and the rest were decimated, six of them dropping in a row. The rest took cover, scattering in all directions.

So far, so good! Sundance leaned against the wall on the right side of the gate and peered into the complex. He wondered if the Soviets would bring up a tank or other big guns. Perhaps, since it was a scientific establishment, the barracks garrison was the only military force on the premises. Even so, those inside could undoubtedly call outside for assistance. Reinforcements might arrive any second.

So what was keeping Blade?

A slug suddenly plowed into the wall next to Sundance's face, and a sliver of stone sliced his left cheek as it exploded from the wall. Sundance spun to the left, and there was a Russian trooper on top of the wall at the other end of the gate. He threw himself backwards as the soldier fired again, then aimed and squeezed the trigger on the FN-50-63. His burst caught the soldier in the abdomen, ripping his guts open, and the Russian screeched as he toppled from the wall to the field below.

They would be closing in now.

Sundance thoughtfully chewed on his lower lip. His position was rapidly becoming untenable.

A faint crackle sounded to the right.

Sundance crouched and whirled, leveling the FN, finding a pair of patrol guards coming at him along the base of the wall. One of them must have accidentally stepped on a twig. He let them have it, hitting the first Russian in the face as the trooper cut loose with an AK-47. The rounds fell short, spraying the dirt at

Sundance's feet. He killed the second guard with several shots to the head.

Where the hell was Blade?

Sundance leaned his back on the wall and hastily ejected the spent magazine from the FN. He slipped in a fresh clip, then glanced into the ministry.

Company was coming.

Four of the soldiers had reached the trees bordering the road, the road winding to the right of the gate, and they were advancing toward the iron gate, going from tree to tree, using the trunks for cover.

Nice move.

Sundance carefully sighted on the foremost soldier, and when the trooper tried to race from one tree to the next, exposing himself for the space of eight feet, Sundance sent a slug into his brain.

The Russian catapulted to the turf between the trees.

The other three halted, all hidden from view.

Sundance hoped his ploy was working. The gunfire must be attracting every guard, every last trooper in the complex. Blade would have a free reign.

What was that?

Sundance twisted to the left, and there was another soldier on top of the wall, trying to fix a bead on him. So he dropped to his knees, and the shot went over his head, missing by mere inches. Sundance was more accurate. His return slug slammed into the soldier's chest and flipped him from the wall, screaming all the way to the ground.

That was close!

Sundance stood and scanned the driveway.

A second trooper was darting from tree to tree.

Idiot!

Sundance aimed and patiently waited for a glimpse of the soldier's head. His bullet tore into the trooper's left cheek and blew out the rear of his cranium, splattering a nearby tree with crimson and fleshy gook.

Sooner or later, one of them would get the range!

Sooner or later.

Sundance inhaled deeply, steadying his nerves. Be vigilant, he told himself. Don't slack off for an instant!

He stiffened as the growl of a motor arose from within the complex. What were they up to now? Bringing up a tank? He scanned the length of road to the right.

It wasn't a tank.

But it was almost as bad.

A jeep containing three troopers and outfitted with a swivel-mounted 50-caliber machine gun was bearing down on the front gate, approaching at a fast clip, the driver weaving the jeep from one side of the road to another, evidently in an effort to present as difficult a target as possible.

The two soldiers sheltered behind the trees opened up with their AK-47's.

Sundance was compelled to duck from sight. He realized what the pair of soldiers were attempting to do. They were keeping him pinned down until the jeep reached the gate. If the jeep could get close enough, there was no way his FN would stand up to the jeep's machine gun.

This was becoming hairy.

Sundance dropped to the ground, onto his stomach, and rolled from cover, his automatic rifle trained on the trees.

The two troopers, concentrating their fire on the wall near the gate, were taken unawares.

Sundance squeezed the trigger, and the first trooper jerked backwards and collapsed. His second round tore through the throat of the other soldier, and the trooper clutched at his ruined neck and fell to his knees, gurgling, blood spurting between his fingers.

The jeep was 50 yards off and closing.

Sundance sighted between two of the iron bars, fixing on a point 30 yards away, a 15-foot tract between two trees.

The soldier manning the machine gun on the jeep cut loose, firing bursts between trees, the barrel of the machine gun elevated to achieve a greater range, but his first shots fell short.

A few rounds struck the edge of the wall, but the majority hit the road near the gate, smacking into the asphalt with a distinct thud-thud-thud.

Sundance waited.

The machine gunner did not spot the man lying prone at the base of the gate. He only knew a sniper was near the front gate, and he was aiming his rounds accordingly, at about waist to chest level, focusing on the edge of the stone wall near the gate. At 40 yards his bursts consistently struck the wall, sending broken bits of stone flying.

Sundance waited.

The jeep roared to within 30 yards of the gate.

Sundance squeezed the trigger and kept it squeezed.

The driver was the initial casualty. A string of ragged dots blossomed on his forehead, and he slumped over the steering wheel. The soldier sitting next to the driver lunged for the wheel, but his head snapped back as he was raked with slugs and flung against the seat. The jeep began slewing across the road, and the machine gunner gripped the machine gun for support as the jeep tilted, then upended, rolling for 20 yards before grinding to a stop in the center of the road. The machine gunner was killed on the first roll, the top of his cranium smashing into the asphalt and splitting like a pulpy rotten tomato.

Sundance rolled to the right, seeking cover behind the wall again. He stood and checked the magazine in the FN. One round left. He tossed it aside and reached for another clip in his pocket.

There were none!

Sundance frowned. That was all he'd brought along. The rest were in the SEAL. Fat good they did him there! But he still had the Grizzlies. He dropped the FN and began unbuttoning his shirt. On the fourth button he paused, gazing at one of the dead gate guards nearby.

The AK-47's!

Sundance darted to the trooper and retrieved the AK-47. The magazine was almost full. He'd never fired one before, but they—

There was a scratching noise above him.

Directly above.

Sundance dived onto his stomach and rolled, and there was a Russian trooper perched on the wall above where he'd been standing.

The soldier blasted four rounds into the ground near the Warrior's head, his AK-47 held extended over the barbed wire.

Sundance returned the fire, lying on his back, the stock of the AK-47 cradled in his right elbow.

A pattern of slugs stitched the soldier on the wall from his crotch to his sternum. He shrieked as he was hurled backwards and disappeared over the rim.

Sundance heard the trooper's body strike the earth on the other side of the wall. He rose and leaned against the stone wall again.

That had been close! Too close!

A resonant voice started shouting orders inside the complex. There was a subdued commotion.

Sundance peered through the gate bars.

The Russians were preparing for an all-out offensive. Dozens of soldiers were crawling across the yard fronting the barracks, and dozens more were following the road, using the trees for protection.

Sundance glanced at the woods beyond the field. The Russians had probably held back at first, unsure of how many attackers were at the gate, saving their main force. By now, they'd learned there was only one man, and they were going to throw everything they had at the iron gate in a concerted effort to end the fray. And Sundance knew he couldn't hold them all off. Not all of them. His best bet was to retreat, to draw them into the woods, buying Blade even more time. If Blade was still alive. A cautious peek verified the Soviets were slowly advancing toward him.

What was that noise?

Sundance cocked his head to the left, listening. It was a strident siren, and he suddenly realized the siren had been blaring for quite a while. In the stress and strain of the combat, he's scarcely noticed.

Several soldiers had reached the demolished jeep.

Sundance took off, angling away from the front gate, heading for the woods. He'd gone only six steps when a startling insight streaked through his mind: if the Soviets were closing in from all directions, from the barracks to the left and the road to the right, *then they must also have troopers closing in on top of the walls!*

They did.

Sundance whirled, the movement saving his life as an AK-47 chattered and sent heavy slugs into the ground near his feet.

The walls were swarming with soldiers!

Sundance raced to the wall as a veritable explosion of gunfire sprayed the earth around him. He placed his back against the wall and looked up. There was a slight lip, or edge, rimming the top of the wall. Attached to metal posts imbedded in the outer edge of the upper surface were coiled strands of barbed wire. In order for the soldiers on the wall to see him, they would need to lean forward over the top strand of barbed wire, exposing themselves to him in the process. If he stayed close to the stone wall, the soldiers up above wouldn't be able to spy him, let alone shoot him. But if he strayed from the wall by so much as 12 inches, the troopers would have a clear line of fire. So he was somewhat safe if he stuck to the wall.

But what about the troops approaching from within the Ministry?

Sundance carefully moved to the end of the wall and looked around the corner.

The nearest soldiers were only 15 yards away.

Sundance sent a short burst in their direction, then fled along the base of the wall.

Someone on the wall was shouting to the soldiers in the complex in Russian.

Go! his mind thundered. Sundance ran for all he was worth. If he could get several hundred yards from the gate, and if the soldiers on the wall and those within the Ministry believed he was still in the vicinity of the gate, they might not notice when he dashed to the woods. On the other hand . . .

There was a lot of yelling on top of the wall.

Sundance imagined the Russians were trying to pinpoint his location. Good. So far, he had them confused. Just a few more seconds was all he needed! His legs pumped rhythmically as he sprinted farther from the iron gate. He dodged the bodies of Bakunin and the two patrol guards and kept going.

An officer on the wall was barking commands.

Sundance exerted himself to the maximum. He discarded the AK-47. Speed was essential, and the AK-47 was too cumbersome and weighty a burden. His arms and legs flying, he covered 40 yards from the front gate, then 60, then 80. He glanced over his right shoulder just as a soldier appeared, and this trooper was followed by several more, coming from within the Ministry.

The Russians had unlocked the gate and opened it!

Sundance immediately swerved to the right, cutting across the field toward the trees, knowing his only hope was in reaching cover before the troopers downed him. He zigzagged, expecting to hear the Ak-47's commence firing any second.

They did.

Sundance was turning to the left, running as crooked a path as possible, when the soldiers on the wall and at the gate were alerted to his maneuver by the shout of a watchful private exiting the complex. Fifteen yards separated Sundance from the woods when the soldiers began firing. Slugs smacked into the grass at his feet. He jagged to the right, followed by a hail of lead. Something stung his left calf and clipped his right shoulder. He focused his total concentration on reaching those trees. Move! He mentally screamed. Move! Move! Move! Four steps to the left, then cut to the right! Five steps to the right, then angle to the left! Never stop! Don't slow down!

He was ten yards from the trees!

A slug dug a furrow in his left side, creasing his ribs, and he nearly stumbled and fell, recovering as he was pitching forward. He made a beeline for the woods. Round after round thumped into the earth all about him.

Five yards!

Sundance took a giant step and executed a spectacular leap, vaulting headfirst into the underbrush and rolling. He came to a jarring stop when his right shoulder collided with a tree.

He'd made it!

But the Russians weren't about to let him escape that easily. Dozens charged from the open gate, fanning out, converging on the trees.

Sundance sat up. His right shoulder was hurting terribly. Through an opening in the brush he saw the troopers approaching in a skirmish line. And all he had were the Grizzlies! He inched around the tree and rose.

What should he do?

Sundance glanced both ways. If he went to the right, back to the jeep, he risked the Russians finding the vehicle and him. Blade would be deprived of the sole means of transportation. But if he went to the left, toward the road leading to the front gate, he'd draw the troopers off, lead them away from the jeep. And eliminate his only hope of escaping.

There was never any doubt.

Sundance moved to the left, reaching under his shirt and drawing the Grizzlies. He silently skirted trees and dry brush, putting more distance between the field and himself.

Some of the troopers reached the woods. Their boots created a pop-crackle-snap cacophony as they clumped through the underbrush. Stealth was forgotten in their eagerness and haste to find their foe. They knew their superior numbers would ultimately flush out their prey.

And so did their quarry. Sundance prudently avoided a dead, brittle limb lying on the dank ground. He caught glimpses of the soldiers now and then. None of them knew he was there.

Yet.

Sundance wondered how far it was to the road. A boulder reared out of the brush, blocking his path. He walked to the left, around the boulder, speculating on his course of action once he reached the road. Preoccupied, he missed hearing the trooper until they nearly bumped into one another as they came around the seven-foot-high boulder at the same moment.

The soldier's mouth dropped, and he frantically leveled his AK-47.

Sundance shot the soldier in the forehead with his left Grizzly.

The trooper's face snapped back as the rear of his head erupted over the nearby vegetation. He tottered and sprawled to the turf.

And all hell broke loose.

Suddenly, soldiers were everywhere, barreling toward the sound of the shot, yelling and shouting, closing in.

Sundance darted in the direction of the road. He could see uniforms here and there, all bearing down on his position.

He was surrounded!

A tall trooper appeared from behind a tree directly ahead.

Sundance fired, his right Grizzly booming, and the trooper was propelled into the tree. He twisted to the left, crashing through a dense thicket, the limbs and thorns tearing at his clothing and skin, and then he was in a small clearing and there were three soldiers coming at him from different directions. He spun to the right and sent a slug into the mouth of the first, beginning his next turn even as he squeezed the trigger, unable to ascertain the effectiveness of the shot, and he plugged the second Russian in the chest and ducked and twirled, and the third trooper was mere yards away and squeezing the trigger on an AK-47. Sundance threw himself to the right, firing as he dove, his shot searing an agonizing path through the third trooper's abdomen. And then Sundance was up and across the clearing and into the trees on the other side.

The forest was alive with bellowed orders and cries.

Sundance heard an AK-47 blaze away to his rear, and his left leg took a hit in the fleshy area of his thigh. His leg nearly buckled, and he staggered and went on, dodging behind a tree and hastening over a low rise.

Another AK-47, somewhere to his right, began shooting.

Sundance swerved to the left, then the right, always heading in the direction of the road. He lost all sense of distance. The road was up ahead, but he had no idea how far it might be, the yardage he'd covered, and he was genuinely surprised when he abruptly plunged from the underbrush and there was the road to the gate, not six feet away.

And soldiers.

Seemingly materializing out of thin air.

Sundance reached the road and bore to the left, going away from the Ministry, hoping his efforts weren't in vain, hoping Blade was accomplishing their mission.

"Freeze!" shouted a stern voice to his right.

Sundance twisted and fired, and a thin trooper doubled over and toppled to the ground. And there was another one, charging from the left, and Sundance pivoted and shot the bastard in the right eye. A pair of soldiers came at him from the rear, firing their AK-47's. Sundance felt a searing spasm lance his right side, but he refused to drop, to submit without expending his last ounce of strength. His body was a blur as he whirled, both Grizzlies thundering, and the two soldiers were slammed to the earth, but another one appeared to take their place, and Sundance shot him in the chest, continuing to rotate, moving, always moving, squeezing both triggers as three soldiers stormed from cover, and two of the Russians twitched and fell but the third wouldn't stop for anything, and Sundance fired as the trooper fired, and fired again as the trooper dropped to his knees, then pitched to the asphalt. Momentarily, Sundance was alone, and he stumbled as dizziness engulfed him. He righted himself with a tremendous effort. How many times had he been hit? He'd lost count. And he'd lost a lot of something else too—blood. His uniform felt clammy and moist, especially the shirt. He lurched a few steps and stopped, reeling. If the Russians found him now, he was a goner.

They found him.

A lone trooper crashed from the underbrush on the left side of the road, swiveling an AK-47 at the crimson-soaked figure in the middle of the asphalt.

And a jeep roared up from out of nowhere, a machine gun blasting, its tires squealing as it barked.

Sundance tried to raise the Grizzlies, but his arms

were enveloped by an overwhelming lethargy. His wounds took belated affect, and with a sigh he sank to the road.

19

Blade threw himself backwards, sweeping his Commando Arms Carbine up and pressing the trigger. The Commando boomed in the narrow stairwell.

The Russian soldier half a flight above was just squeezing the trigger of his AK-47 when the Commando's slugs tore through his face and flung him to the stairs. The AK-47 fell from his lifeless fingers, rattling as it slid down several steps.

Blade hesitated, getting his bearings. He had entered Penza Hall on the ground level, then descended three levels to the lowest floor. The guard had led him up three floors from the bottom level, which meant he should be on ground level again.

There was only one way to find out.

There were two doors furnishing access to the stairwell. The one he'd just used, and another, the one which should lead to the loading dock. Blade opened the second door and found the hallway he needed.

And a trooper jogging toward him with an AK-47 at the ready.

Blade shot the startled soldier, sending a burst into the trooper's chest and flipping him to the floor. He sprinted toward the door to the loading dock. The laundry truck was probably gone. He would need to improvise another method of departing the Ministry. As he opened the door to the dock, the sound of the siren rose in volume. Another noise blended with the sirens; the repeated blasting of gunfire.

Sundance?

Blade scanned the loading dock and the parking lot. There wasn't a vehicle in sight.

Damn!

Blade ran down the ramp to the lot and started across, bearing toward the west wall. If the clamor was any accurate indication, then a war was being waged near the west wall. He hurried, the Commando in his right hand.

A squad of soldiers unexpectedly came into view to the left.

Blade slowed, expecting to be challenged. But the squad leader gave him a cursory inspection and continued on, hastening in the direction of the front gate. Off to the north, more soldiers were jogging toward the gate.

If it was Sundance out there, he wouldn't be able to hold them off for long!

Blade bounded across the lot in mighty strides, reaching a lawn encircling a lofty structure. He bypassed the edifice to the south, heading away from the gate. If every soldier in the Ministry was converging on the front gate, then he might be able to sneak over the wall near the southwest corner. He darted around a huge maple tree.

A Russian soldier, a big man with wide shoulders, was ten yards off, jogging to the northwest.

Blade slowed, hoping he wouldn't be spotted.

The soldier glanced to the right and halted, his forehead creasing in perplexity. An AK-47 was slung over his right shoulder. "You!" he barked.

Blade touched his chest with his left hand. "Me?"

"Yes, you! Come here!" the soldier ordered.

Blade walked over to the soldier. "Yes?"

"Yes, sergeant!" the Russian corrected him. The sergeant's brown eyes critically examined the giant's uniform. "Where are you going?" he queried.

"To the wall," Blade responded. "Sergeant!"

The sergeant pointed to the north. "But the action is that way! Everyone is to assemble at the gate. Why are you going in the opposite direction?"

"Orders," Blade replied.

"Orders. From whom?" the sergeant inquired. He began to unsling his AK-47.

Blade knew the sergeant didn't believe him, knew the noncom wasn't unlimbering the AK-47 for the exercise. He couldn't afford to be detained, not if Sundance was in jeopardy. He did the only thing he could do, under the circumstances. He kicked the sergeant in the nuts.

The Russian doubled over, gasping, his hands covering his genitals, his mouth forming a wide oval.

Blade rammed the Commando barrel into the noncom's mouth and fired.

The sergeant's brains gushed from the rear of his cranium, and he was hurled to the grass, convulsing, his eyes glazing.

Blade resumed his dash to the left wall. A quick scan confirmed no one else was in the area.

The siren wailed and wailed.

The battle near the gate raged on.

Blade came within sight of the wall. To his left, perhaps 40 yards distant, a flight of steps led up to the top of the wall. One soldier was visible, and he was moving along the top of the wall toward the front gate. Blade slanted in the direction of those steps. He could feel the stolen KGB files rubbing against his skin, and the Bowie scabbards brushing his thighs.

Yells and shouts were coming from the northwest.

What if the cause of the commotion wasn't Sundance? Blade asked himself. But if not Sundance, then who? The Packrats? No. They apparently confined their activities to Valley Forge and vicinity. Were there rebels active in the occupied zone? Freedom fighters opposing the Soviets? If so, the Freedom Federation would need to contact them and arrange aid. He reached the bottom of the steps, discarding all speculation as he sped to the top of the wall.

Soldiers could be seen off to the north, atop the wall near the gate. But none were nearby.

A four-foot-high barrier of barbed wire separated Blade from the field below. He gingerly touched one of the coiled strands, and his third finger was pricked by a sharp barb. The inner rampart was two feet below the wire. There was a six-inch lip, or rim, on both sides of the wire. By stepping up onto the rim, and balancing himself precariously, he was able to lean over the wire and survey the field and the woods.

Not a trooper anywhere.

Blade elevated his left leg, raising it over the barbed wire and placing his left foot on the outer rim. The barbed wire scraped his crotch, and he envisioned the impaling he would suffer if he slipped. Goose bumps broke out on his gonads. Holding the wire down with his left hand, he carefully eased his right leg up and over. For a second he perched on the outer rim, gazing at the ground 15 feet below. Then he launched himself into the air, dropping feet first, the air whipping his hair, and he landed and rolled, rising and running toward the woods.

No one challenged him.

Blade reached the trees and plunged into the brush. He bore to the right, seeking the jeep. The jeep was hidden near the turnoff, 60 yards from the road leading to the gate. After what seemed like an eternity, he parted the tall weeds before him and there was the turnoff. But which way was the jeep? Was he too far south or north? Acting on a hunch, he turned to the right, to the north, and within 15 yards discovered the field he wanted. He sprinted into the brush, smiling when he spotted the jeep. But his smile quickly changed to a frown when he reached the driver's door and peered inside.

Bakunin was gone!

Blade straightened, scanning the landscape. What the hell had happened? Had Bakunin loosened his bounds? Had the captain gone to warn the Ministry? Had Sundance seen Bakunin? Was that the reason for the combat near the gate? Suddenly, all the pieces to the puzzle fit. If Sundance had observed Bakunin heading for the front gate, Sundance would have stopped him. And now Sundance was in mortal danger, resisting impossible odds, and all because Bakunin had been left alive. Blade grimaced. If Sundance was seriously injured, or worse, it was all his fault. He should have executed the officer, not spared the Russian. Plato's philosophy was too idealistic for the real world, too compassionate for a seasoned Warrior. He had known it all along! Blade fumed. Anger washed over him, anger at his own stupidity. He removed his keys from his pocket and climbed in, placing the Commando to his right, gunning the engine, and flooring the pedal as he shifted into reverse.

The jeep's tires sent clumps of dirt and vegetation soaring as the tread dug into the turf.

Blade glanced over his right shoulder, steering the jeep backwards in a tight loop. He shifted into gear, and the jeep surged across the field to the turnoff. Spinning the wheel, Blade turned to the right, making for the road to the gate. He traveled 20 yards, when he happened to look in the rearview mirror.

Three motorcycles were roaring up the highway behind him.

Where did the turnoff lead to? Blade wondered. He drove the jeep to the shoulder of the road and braked, grabbing the Commando.

The cycles were 20 yards away, on the other side of the street, obviously intending to swing around the jeep as they raced to the intersection with the road to the gate, 40 yards to the north. Each rider was a Soviet soldier wearing a black helmet.

Blade hastily rolled down his window and lifted the Commando barrel as the three motorcycles came abreast of the jeep. The Commando thundered, and the hapless drivers were rocked by a withering hail of lead. Two of the bikes wobbled, them smashed together, hurtling to the far side of the street in a tangle of crushed limbs and twisted metal. They slammed into a tree, breaking into bits and pieces.

The third biker survived the ambush. He was nicked in the right arm, and his bike wavered for a few yards, then steadied as the rider slewed to a screeching halt 20 yards in front of the jeep. He drew an automatic pistol from a holster on his left hip.

Blade waited for the biker to make the first move.

The cyclist suddenly turned his handle bars and

accelerated, making for the intersection.

Blade mashed the gas pedal and the jeep sped in pursuit. The motorcyle was faster, closing on the intersection at a reckless speed. Blade knew he couldn't catch the biker. And he also knew the rider would take a right, heading for the Ministry. He transferred the Commando to his left hand, steering with his right. Poking the barrel out the window, he angled the automatic in the direction of the intersection. The jeep was a mere 18 yards from the junction when the motorcycle swung into the turn. Blade depressed the trigger and held it down, the Commando bucking as he fired. For a second or two, he believed he'd missed, miscalculated the range and the elevation.

The biker was smoothly negotiating the turn, his cycle slanted, his body tucked close to the bike. His front tire abruptly exploded as four slugs shredded the rubber, and the motorcycle was catapulted forward, turning end over end, throwing the biker to the side, his spindly form smashing into the asphalt and rolling for a good ten yards, his arms and legs flopping and flapping. He came to rest on the right shoulder, his helmet cracked, his left leg bent at an unnatural posture, immobile.

Blade reached the intersection and took a right. His keen eyes probed the road ahead, and narrowed as he spied the stumbling figure in the blood-drenched uniform.

It was Sundance!

Blade tramped on the gas, his right hand tightening on the steering wheel until his knuckles turned white. He could see a lot of bodies lining the road.

A trooper suddenly shoved through the underbrush, aiming an AK-47 at Sundance.

Blade thumped on the brake, swerving the jeep so his side faced the trooper, shoving the Commando out the window and squeezing the trigger.

The soldier was perforated from his knees to his shoulders. He twisted and fell, rivulets of crimson seeping from the holes.

Blade clutched at the shift as the jeep began to lurch, and he shifted into park and leaped to the ground.

Sundance had collapsed!

Blade reached his friend in three bounds. He knelt, appalled by all the blood.

Boots pounded to his right.

Blade spun as a soldier emerged from the woods. The Commando boomed, ripping the soldier in half at the waist.

Upraised voices bellowed in the forest.

Blade swiftly slung the Commando over his left arm, and gently placed his forearms under Sundance. He lifted, hardly straining, and carried his fellow Warrior to the jeep. He was compelled to hurry, knowing the Russians were closing in, but he was reluctant to jostle Sundance.

"This way!" someone called off to the left.

Blade yanked the passenger door open, and solicitously deposted Sundance in the seat. He closed the door, moved around to the driver's side, and hopped in. The jeep's motor purred as he shifted and performed a U-turn, gathering speed, racing away from the Ministry of Psychological Sciences.

Soldiers poured from the woods to the rear. Some fired their AK-47's ineffectively.

Sundance slumped forward until his forehead rested on the dash. His chin drooped onto his chest, and his body swayed with every bump in the road.

Blade glanced at his companion, emotionally tormented. This was his doing! He knew it! The result of his incompetence! The mission had been a total washout! First Bertha had vanished, and now this! And all for what? The captured Vikings were all dead, leaving the Family with several files and the lingering hope of a possible alliance. Were the files worth the lives of two Warriors?

"Hang in there," Blade said to the unconscious figure beside him. "Don't you die on me, damnit!"

Sundance sagged to the floor.

20

"There they are!" Cole whispered.

Bertha and the three Claws were concealed behind four trees on the crest of a hill five miles to the south of the log cabin.

"It's the Bobcats!" Eddy exclaimed. "I knew it!"

Bertha, her left shoulder pressed against the rough bark of an elm tree, watched 11 Bobcats 75 yards below her position. They were following a faint deer trail winding along the base of the hill. Eight were boys, 3 girls. They ranged in ages from about 10 to 16 or 17. Like the Claws, their clothing consisted of tattered rags. They were smiling, joking with one another, evidently happy over their presumed defeat of the Claws.

"Look at the sons of bitches!" Cole snapped. He stood behind a pine tree to Bertha's right.

"Let's get the scum!" Eddy stated from his spot to Bertha's left, crouched near another elm.

"What's that big gun?" Libby asked. She was standing next to a pine on Cole's right.

Bertha was asking herself the same question. It was a huge machine gun, mounted on a tripod, and it took four Bobcats to carry the weapon, tripod and all. The Bobcats must have swiped the machine gun from the Russians and decided to use it on their enemies, the Claws.

"Who cares what it is?" Cole retorted. "It won't stop us from wasting those creeps."

The corners of Bertha's mouth turned downward. She didn't like this. Didn't like it one bit. It was all well and good to talk about teaching the Bobcats a lesson. But it was another matter to seriously contemplate shooting a 10-year-old. Or 11. Or 12. Try as she might, Bertha could only view the Bobcats in one light: as children. Savage little murderers, perhaps, but still children. She compared them to the children at the

Home. The difference was incredible. The Family's children were taught to reverence all life, to exalt love as the highest form of personal expression, and to strive for an inner communion with the Spirit. The Packrats, whether it was the Bobcats, the Claws, or any of the other gangs, by contrast had reduced all life to the primitive level of kill-or-be-killed. They didn't have the slightest idea of the true nature of mature love. And of spiritual affairs they were pitifully ignorant. The disparity was like night and day. It was amazing, Bertha reflected, the difference the Family and the Home made in the lives of the children. She suddenly became aware Cole was addressing her.

" . . . us or not?" Cole demanded.

Bertha turned. "What did you say?"

"I want to know if you're with us or not?" Cole repeated.

Bertha glanced at the Bobcats. "I don't know," she confessed.

"I thought you were on our side!" pudgy Eddy interjected.

"I am," Bertha said. "But . . ." She paused, uncertain.

"But what?" Cole pressed her.

"But I don't think I could kill the Bobcats," Bertha stated, nodding toward the base of the hill.

"Why not?" Libby inquired.

"They're just kids!" Bertha declared. "Look at 'em! Half of 'em aren't much over twelve!" She frowned, staring at Cole. "I'm sorry. I just can't do it."

Surprisingly, Cole shrugged. "Suit yourself. You stay here, then."

Bertha leaned toward the Claw chief. "Why don't you forget about this vengeance bit? One of you could get hurt, or even killed. Drop it, Cole. Come back to the Home with me."

Cole averted his eyes. "I can't," he said.

"You could if you wanted to," Bertha prompted him.

Cole stared at Bertha, his expression one of profound sorrow. "I can't," he reiterated, and motioned to Eddy and Libby. He moved from cover and started down the slope.

Eddy winked at Bertha, then followed Cole.

Libby stepped over to Bertha. "I'll miss you," she stated sadly.

"Don't do it!" Bertha said. "Please!"

"I've got to go," Libby asserted. "I can't let Cole and Eddy do it alone."

"Talk to Cole some more," Bertha suggested. "You can talk him out of it, if anyone can!"

"I can't," Libby said. "I've already tried."

"Try again!" Bertha urged. "What harm can it do?"

"It's no use," Libby insisted.

"How do you know. What makes you so damn sure?" Bertha asked.

Libby looked into Bertha's eyes. "Milly was Cole's sister." She whirled and dashed after Cole and Eddy.

His sister! Bertha sagged against the elm. Sweet little Milly had been Cole's sister! No wonder he was out for blood! Bertha watched the three Claws cautiously descend the hill. She'd never even considered some of the Packrats might be related. But how else would the younger ones have made it to Valley Forge, unless they were accompanied by an older brother or sister?

Cole and Eddy had halted and were waiting for Libby. Cole glanced up once at Bertha and smiled wanly.

Libby reached them, and together they continued their descent, utilizing the trees, boulders, and weeds as cover as they crept ever nearer to the unsuspecting Bobcats.

Bertha felt queasy in her stomach. Lordy! She had a *bad* feeling about this!

Cole, Eddy, and Libby reached a maple tree 60 yards from the bottom of the hill.

Bertha didn't want to watch, but she couldn't bring herself to tear her eyes away. Indecision racked her soul. What if she was wrong? What if she should be helping the Claws? They'd befriended her, hadn't they? Spared her, when they could have killed her? Back at the cabin, she'd believed she was partly to blame for the butchery committed on the other Claws. Now, she wasn't so sure. She was torn between her desire to aid her friends, and her repugnance at the mere thought of killing a child.

The three Claws attained a boulder 40 yards from the Bobcats, still undetected by their quarry.

Bertha scrutinized the Bobcats. They were strung out over a 20-yard stretch of trail. The quartet bearing the heavy machine gun was bringing up the rear, at least ten feet behind the rest. The apparent leader, a tall youth with black hair, armed with an AK-47, was about five feet in front of the group. AK-47's were the standard weapon, except for two boys who were toting rifles.

Bertha tensed as she saw Cole, Libby and Eddy creep to within 20 yards of the Bobcats. They crouched behind a spreading pine. Cole wagged his hand to the right and the left, and Eddy and Libby started off in the corresponding directions.

The Bobcat leader unexpectedly paused, scanning the hill.

Bertha held her breath.

Cole, Libby, and Eddy froze in their tracks.

The Bobcat leader looked over his shoulder at the gang, then resumed his journey.

Bertha took a deep breath.

Cole, Libby, and Eddy were crawling down the hill, silently parting the brush in their path, stopping whenever a Bobcat idly gazed up the hill.

The Bobcat leader halted beside a maple tree and leaned down, doing something with his right shoe.

Cole was now within 10 yards of the Bobcats, close to the center of their column. Libby was 12 yards from the four carrying the machine gun. And pudgy Eddy was 12 yards from the Bobcat leader.

What were they waiting for? Bertha craned her neck for a better view. The Claws should strike before the . . .

Cole suddenly rose to his feet from a clump of weeds, his AK-47 leveled. "You slime!" he shouted, and fired.

Three of the Bobcats in the middle of the line were ripped to pieces by the automatic barrage, the slugs slamming into their bodies and exploding out their backs, ravaging their torsos. Their limbs jerked and flapped as they were struck and knocked to the ground.

The other Bobcats lunged for the nearest cover.

Libby popped up from behind a log, and her sweeping spray of lead caught the four with the machine gun in their chests. They died in midstride, crumpling under the weight of the machine gun.

Eddy rose, aiming at the Bobcat leader.

Only the Bobcat leader was quicker. He must have sensed something was wrong, must have been toying with his shoe as a ruse, because he was already in motion as Eddy stood, and both fired at the same instant.

Eddy's head snapped back, a crimson geyser erupting from his left ear, and he toppled to the grass.

The Bobcat leader ducked behind the maple tree.

Bertha started to raise the M-16, but hesitated. No! She wouldn't—she couldn't—shoot children!

Cole dropped another Bobcat, and then flattened. Libby did likewise.

The three remaining Bobcats were raking the hillside with gunfire, shooting in the general direction of their adversaries.

From her vantage point high on the hill, Bertha saw Cole's left shoulder twist sharply, as if he had been hit.

The firing abated, each side waiting for the other to make the next move. In addition to the Bobcat leader, a girl of 14 or 15 and a boy approximately the same age were the only Bobcats still alive. The girl was hidden in a cluster of boulders 20 yards from Libby, and the boy was concealed in a thicket less than 15 yards from Cole.

Bertha could see Cole and Libby clearly. The Bobcat girl was visible every now and then, whenever she popped her head up for a quick look-see. Although Bertha knew where the Bobcat leader and the other boy were hiding, neither betrayed their position, neither appeared in her field of view.

Cole was tentatively groping his left side, and when he drew his right hand aside, his fingers were dripping blood.

Bertha nervously bit her lower lip. She was in an agonizing quandary. If she didn't do something, do *anything,* and fast, Cole might die. But what could she do, short of shooting a Bobcat?

Libby was on her hands and knees, sheltered by a log, trying to peek around the end of the log and spot Cole.

Bertha doubted whether Libby could see Cole. He was too well camouflaged by a stand of weeds.

Cole was checking the magazine of his AK-47.

Bertha finally made up her mind. Just because she felt uncomfortable about killing a Bobcat didn't mean she couldn't aid the Claws in another manner. As a distraction, for instance. If she could attract the Bobcat's attention, she might provide Cole and Libby with the openings they needed. The idea was worth a try. She began moving down the hill, crouched over, treading lightly.

Libby was now on her knees, continuing to scan for Cole.

Don't do anything stupid! Bertha almost yelled. She skirted a blue spruce. So how, she asked herself, was she going to help Cole and Libby without getting herself shot? The Bobcats would shoot at anything they saw moving. She had to be extremely careful.

Cole had squirmed onto his elbows and knees.

What was he up to? Bertha halted behind a rock outcropping 60 yards from the base of the hill.

There was movement in the thicket secreting the Bobcat boy.

Bertha stiffened. She was too far away yet! If only nothing would happen until she was closer! She scrambled forward on her stomach, across a grassy stretch, and reached a maple tree. Once behind the trunk, she stood and surveyed the situation below.

The movement in the thicket had ceased.

Libby was still seeking a glimpse of Cole.

Cole was peering over the top of the weeds.

Bertha was about to crouch and proceed further, when something flickered at the edge of her vision, lower down and off to the right. She glanced in that direction, her nerves tingling.

The Bobcat leader had circled around Cole! He was 15 yards from Cole's hiding place, slowly advancing, stooped over.

How the hell had he done it? Bertha had supposed he was on the opposite side of the tree where he'd taken cover. The guy was good! There was no doubt about it.

The Bobcat leader was searching from side to side. Several trees and a dense bush separated him from Cole.

Bertha didn't believe the Bobcat leader had seen Cole. Yet. But in a few seconds Cole was bound to be spotted. Her eyes narrowed as she watched the Bobcat leader, waiting for the right moment. He passed one of the trees, then another. Bertha's abdomen tightened expectantly. The tall Bobcat leader came abreast of the third tree, and now just the bush obscured Cole's hiding place from the alert, black-haired youth. Bertha's eyes were glued to the Bobcat's ragged brown leather shoes. He took one step, then another, cautiously edging around the bush to the left. Another one took him to the very border of the bush. He was scrutinizing the slope above him, and he still hadn't spied Cole squatting in the weeds. He raised his leg, about to go past the bush, and as he did, Bertha took her calculated gamble. She leaped from concealment, waving her arms. "Up here, turkey!" she shouted.

The Bobcat leader swiveled at the sound of her voice, pointing his AK-47 up the hill.

Even as the Bobcat leader was turning, Cole spun too. He saw the leader's head and shoulders visible above the bush, and he fired from a crouch, his burst striking the Bobcat leader in the face and flinging the tall youth to the turf.

And suddenly, everything went wrong.

Libby, hearing the gunfire but unable to see Cole, sprang to her feet, anxious for his safety, heedless of her own. It was a fatal mistake.

The Bobcat girl in the boulders jumped up, blasting from the hip, her AK-47 on full automatic.

Libby was hurled onto her back by the impact, her arms spreading wide.

Cole whirled at the chatter of the Bobcat girl's weapon, and he saw Libby get hit. He surged from cover, crashing through the underbrush toward Libby. *"No!"* he screamed. *"No! No!"*

The Bobcat in the thicket abruptly stepped into view, aiming a rifle at Cole, and he squeezed the trigger as Cole recklessly crossed a small clearing five yards from Libby.

Cole stumbled as he was struck. He twirled toward the Bobcat in the thicket, and he fired as the Bobcat's rifle thundered again, and kept firing as the Bobcat doubled over and dropped to one side. He turned toward Libby, staggering haltingly.

The Bobcat girl in the boulders pressed her AK-47 to her right shoulder, aiming at Cole.

All of this transpired so swiftly, so unexpectedly, Bertha reacted belatedly. Four seconds elapsed between her shout and Cole being struck, and when she did act, when she did enter the fray, her action was instinctive, ingrained from years of gang warfare and her training as a Warrior. Caught up in the heat of the moment, fearing for Cole and Libby, she did the only thing she could have done under the circumstances. She saw the Bobcat girl aim at Cole, and she automatically sighted her M-16 and fired off a half-dozen rounds.

The shots were right on target. The Bobcat girl stiffened, then sprawled over a boulder.

Bertha plunged down the slope, taking the straightest route, limbs and thorns tearing at her clothes. Her left boot snagged in a root and she tripped, landing on both knees. But she was up in an instant, plowing through the vegetation, and she didn't stop until she reached the small clearing near Libby. She halted in midstep, horrified, her countenance reflecting her emotional unheaval. "Dear Lord!" she exclaimed.

Cole was on his knees in the middle of the clearing, his right arm outstretched toward Libby. His body was trembling, and blood coated the front of his brown shirt. His green eyes were locked on Libby.

Libby's green shift was crimson from the waist up. Bullet holes dotted the fabric. She was flat on her back, her right arm extended toward Cole, her brown eyes staring at him in acute misery. Their fingers were a mere inch apart.

Cole made a valiant effort to rise, to move closer to Libby, but his legs buckled, and he sagged to his knees.

Libby's gaze shifted, focused on Bertha. "Please!" she pleaded. "Please!"

Bertha hurried over to Cole, slinging the M-16 over her left arm.

Cole tried to twist, to use the AK-47 in his left hand, detecting movement but unaware of Bertha's proximity.

"It's me! Bertha!" Bertha informed him, reaching his side and placing her right arm around his waist.

Cole turned his tormented face toward her. "Help me," he said. "Must touch Libby."

Bertha nodded. She heaved, lifting him, assisting him to move next to Libby. She could feel his blood trickling over her arm.

Cole wearily knelt alongside Libby. Bertha released him, and he almost toppled over. Weaving, he dropped the AK-47 and braced himself with his left arm. He smiled down at Libby.

Libby beamed up at him.

Bertha stood at Libby's feet, her eyes moistening.

"Looks like I made a mess of things," Cole said, his voice barely audible.

Libby was breathing heavily. "No, you didn't," she admonished him. "We did okay."

"You always were one for looking at the bright side of things," Cole remarked, and coughed.

Libby glanced at Bertha. "Did we get them? Did we get all of them?"

"Yes," Bertha answered softly.

"See?" Libby grinned at Cole. "We paid them back for Milly and the others. We did okay."

Cole nodded once, his eyelids fluttering. "I guess we did, at that."

Libby's right hand drifted to Cole's lap.

Cole took her hand in his, their fingers entwining. Tears filled his eyes. "I'm sorry, Libby."

"For what?"

"For all the time I wasted. I heard you talking to Bertha outside the cabin." He paused, coughed some more. "I'm sorry for not showing you how I felt. I'm sorry for all the time we could have shared. I'm sorry because I was scared to tell you, scared to open up, scared of losing you. You were right." He grimaced and coughed, and blood appeared at the left corner of his mouth.

"We'll be together again," Libby assured him. She seemed to be staring dreamily into the distance. "I told you about my mom lots of times, about how nice she was. She was very religious, even though religion is against the law. Maybe that's why the Russians took Dad and her. She used to read to us from the Bible, tell us about Jesus and God and Heaven. Heaven is a wonderful place. Nobody tries to kill you there. You always have enough to eat. And there's lots of angels all over, and music, music with harps and singing and all. And love. Everybody loves everybody. Isn't that great?"

Blood was seeping from both corner's of Cole's mouth. "You think," he began, and wheezed, "you think we'll go to this Heaven?"

Libby looked him in the eyes. "Yes, I do."

Cole's features were blancing. "I don't know . . ."

"Tell him, Bertha," Libby said. "Tell him."

Bertha found it difficult to speak. "I don't know much about God and such," she confessed.

Libby frowned.

"But the folks at the Home do," Bertha quickly added. "The Elders there say we live on after this life. They say we go to a better place, a higher spiritual level they call it."

Cole took a deep breath. "And how . . . do we get to this better place?"

"The Elders say all it takes is faith," Bertha stated, recalling several worship services she'd attended. "All you got to do is believe in the Spirit."

"I believe," Libby declared weakly. She gazed at Cole. "Please. For me. Believe."

Cole coughed and slumped lower. "I never gave it much . . . thought before." He paused. "But if it means I'll see you again, then for you"—he wheezed—"I'll believe."

Libby gripped his hand tightly. "Thank you." She looked up at a patch of sky visible through the trees. "I can't wait to get there! Maybe we'll see our parents again. Wouldn't that be fantastic?"

Cole didn't answer.

"Cole?" Libby said, alarmed, examining his rigid features.

Cole was quivering. He began to droop forward, his eyes on her. "I . . . love . . . you," he said, and collapsed across her waist.

Bertha took a step nearer and reached for Cole.

"Don't!" Libby stated.

"But . . ." Bertha started to protest.

"Leave him," Libby directed. "I want him like this." She managed to move her left hand to his head and began stroking his hair. For a minute she was quiet, frowning. Then she mustered a wan smile. "You know, this is the first time I've touched him like this. I can't believe it!"

Bertha felt light-headed.

"Bertha?" Libby said. Her voice was fading.

"I'm here," Bertha assured her huskily.

"Promise me something," Libby stated.

"Anything."

"Promise me you'll bury us side by side. Hand in hand. Please? I don't want the animals to get us," Libby said.

Bertha responded with the utmost difficulty. "I promise you. I'll bury you side by side."

"Thank you." Libby gazed up at the sky, and an incredible expression of happiness transformed her face. "We're on our way!" she cried, elated. She gasped once, then ceased breathing.

An eerie silence enshrouded the hillside, until an unusual sound arose from a small clearing near the base of the hill, a sound gaining in intensity as it continued, softly at first, and then in loud, moanful sobs, the sound of a Warrior crying.

21

The day was cold, the sky a bright blue. He was dressed all in gray, with a pair of Grizzlies nestled in shoulder holsters, one under each arm. The Family firing range was all his. Few Family members ventured into the southeastern corner of the Home. The children were instructed to stay away from the firing range, which consisted of a large clearing with an earth bank at the east end. The Warriors used the firing range regularly, and the other Family members were required to visit it periodically to take firing lessons under the Warriors' tutelage, to familiarize themselves with the correct use of firearms in case the Home ever sustained another assault.

Two rusted tin cans had been placed on the earthen bank.

He draped his arms at his sides, shook his head to relax the muscles, and drew, the Grizzlies gleaming as they flashed from their holsters. Both pistols boomed, and the tin cans flipped into the air. They dropped to the dirt and rattled to the bottom of the bank.

"Right smart shootin', Sundance," remarked someone behind him.

Sundance recognized the voice. He slid the Grizzlies into their holsters and turned. "I've been expecting you," he said.

The blond gunman in the buckskins nodded. "Figured as much." He indicated the bank with a wave of his right hand. "It looks like you're pretty much healed."

Sundance glanced at the tin cans. "Just about. It's been a tough two months," he admitted.

"I know," the man in the buckskins stated. "I've been keepin' tabs on you, checkin' with the Healers every now and then. They told me you likely would've died if Bertha hadn't tended you on the way back from Philly. They said it was touch and go for a spell. You must be one tough hombre, Sundance."

Sundance studied the Family's legendary gunfighter. "And to what do I owe all this attention, Hickok?"

Hickok grinned, his blond mustache curling upward. "I reckon you know why I'm here."

It was Sundance's turn to nod. "I guess I do. And I don't see where it's any business of yours."

Hickok's grin faded. "I'm making it my business," he declared.

Sundance felt his temper rise. "You shouldn't butt your nose in where it doesn't belong."

Hickok hooked his thumbs in his gunbelt. "That's where you're wrong, pard. I do have a legitimate stake in what's going on. One of my best buddies, Blade, and one of the people I care for a whole bunch, Bertha, came back from the Philly run all discombobulated. And do you know what the reason was?"

"What?" Sundance responded.

"You," Hickok said.

"How do you figure?" Sundance queried defensively.

"Blade can be a moody cuss at times," Hickok commented. "And he moped around here for weeks after you three got back. It took Geronimo and me a while to pry the reason out of him, but he finally 'fessed up to bein' upset over what happened to you. It had something to do with some Commie captain. Blade blamed himself for you bein' hurt. Claimed it never would've happened if he'd done what he should've done with the captain."

"It wasn't Blade's fault," Sundance said.

"Well, Blade ain't content unless he can blame himself for everything that goes wrong in his life,"

Hickok mentioned, and chuckled. "Sometimes I swear the big dummy would blame himself for bad weather, if he could get away with it. Luckily for him, he's got his missus, Geronimo, and me to keep him in line. He got over what happened to you." Hickok paused. "But Bertha is another story."

"Bertha doesn't concern you," Sundance stated.

Hickok was standing ten feet away. He moved closer, his hands straying to his sides. "Bertha *does* concern me, pard. A lot. We go back a long way. We've been through a lot together. We were close friends before the two of you ever met. Like I said, I care for her. And I get a mite ticked off when some yahoo gives her a bum steer!"

"Bum steer?" Sundance snapped angrily. "Who the hell do you think you are? If Bertha has something to say to me, let her say it to my face! She doesn't need to send you to do her talking for her!"

"She didn't send me," Hickok said.

"Then why are you here?" Sundance demanded. "Bertha and I are adults. We don't need you to play matchmaker!"

Hickok pursed his lips, then sighed. "I can see you want to do this the hard way."

"We have nothing to discuss," Sundance reiterated. "Get lost."

Hickok squared his shoulders. "Why don't you make me?"

Sundance tensed. "Don't push me," he warned.

"Or what?" Hickok asked. "You'll draw on me?"

"I'll only be pushed so far," Sundance declared. "I don't like it when someone meddles in my personal affairs."

"You didn't answer my question," Hickok noted. "You goin' to draw on me?"

"I won't draw on a fellow Warrior," Sundance said.

Hickok smirked. "Ahhh. Ain't that sweet! Tell you what I'll do. You say you want me to get lost?"

"That's right," Sundance affirmed.

"Then you beat me on the draw," Hickok proposed,

"and I'll make tracks."

"What?"

"That's right. You beat me, and I get lost. I beat you, and you hear me out. What do you say?" Hickok prompted him.

"You're crazy!" Sundance exclaimed.

Hickok shrugged. "Everybody knows that. Now what about it? Do we have a deal?"

"I beat you," Sundance said, "and you promise you'll take a hike?"

"You have my word," Hickok vowed. "All you have to do is get a bead on my belly button before I get one on yours, and I'm out of your life."

Sundance mulled over the proposition. He was genuinely annoyed at Hickok for prying into his private life, and he resented Hickok's smug attitude. Ordinarily, he detested exhibitionism. But this was a special case. He wanted to teach Hickok a lesson.

"What's it goin' to be?" Hickok asked. "Yes or no?"

"I'll do it!" Sundance declared. "And then I want you to get the hell out of here!"

"Such a mouth for a Warrior!" Hickok quipped. "Ain't you heard we're supposed to set an example for the younguns?"

"Let's get this nonsense over with," Sundance commented acidly.

"Touchy sort, huh?" Hickok shrugged. "Okay. To do this fair, let's both hold our arms straight out from our sides. Like this." He raised his arms.

"This is ridiculous," Sundance said, elevating his arms.

Hickok surveyed the clearing and the surrounding forest. "Do you see that sparrow over there?" he inquired.

Sundance glanced to his right. "That one on top of the pine tree?"

"That's the one," Hickok confirmed. "When it takes off, we slap leather."

"We draw when the bird flies off?" Sundance said.

"That's the general notion," Hickok declared.

"That's stupid," Sundance complained.

"You got a better idea?"

"No," Sundance reluctantly replied.

"Then when the sparrow skedaddles," Hickok directed, "pull your irons."

Sundance concentrated on the bird. He suddenly viewed the outcome of their mock duel as extremely important. He wanted, more than anything else, to put Hickok in his place. He was tired of always being compared to the Family's supreme gunfighter. And he wanted to prove he was a skilled pistoleer in his own right.

A minute dragged by.

Two.

Sundance could feel his shoulder muscles beginning to ache.

The sparrow stayed perched on the tree, chirping contentedly, enjoying the sunshine.

Sundance felt a twinge in his right shoulder, and he remembered the cautionary advice the Healers had given him, not to strain his shoulder or he would spend another week in the infirmary. If the damn bird didn't move soon, he'd have to for—

The sparrow took wing.

Sundance drew like never before, his hands streaking to his holsters, the Grizzlies flying free and sweeping low, the barrels already aimed, and then, and only then, did he realize *Hickok hadn't drawn!* He froze, utterly dumfounded.

Hickok laughed. "I never draw on a fellow Warrior either," he explained. "And I'm goin' to speak my piece, whether you like it or not."

Sundance absently stared at the Grizzlies in his hands, then at Hickok.

"Bertha has been alone for a long, long time," Hickok was saying. "Too long. Once, way back when, she told me she wanted us to be an item. You've got to admire her grit!" Hickok paused, his tone softening. "I felt real bad about it, 'cause I never seriously looked at her as more than a friend. A close friend. One of the best. And when I met Sherry, it cinched things for me. I know there's been a lot of gossip about Bertha and me. Some people ain't got nothin' better to do with their time than flap their gums!" He stared at his moccasins. "But I wanted you to know there isn't any truth to those lousy rumors. And I wanted to ask you something, man to man. Warrior to Warrior."

Sundance noticed Hickok was using a normal vocabulary. "What is it?"

Hickok gazed into Sundance's eyes. "How you feel about Bertha is your business. But if you do have any feelings for her, any feelings at all, then why don't you go talk to her? I know you've hardly said three words to her since you got back from Philly. I'm not even going to ask you why. That's your business too. But if you do like her, even just a little bit, why don't you get to know her? I guarantee you'll never find a better woman, anywhere."

"Why are you doing this?" Sundance asked. "If she wants to talk to me, then why didn't she visit me in the infirmary?"

"I'm doin' this 'cause I'm a busybody," Hickok answered. "And 'cause Blade said Bertha was actin' like she's interested in you. I don't know why she didn't come see you when you were laid up. She's kept pretty much to herself since you three came back. I think something happened to her out there. I don't know what. That's for you to find out. If you want to, that is." Hickok grinned and started to turn. "There. I've said my fill. The rest is up to you. And if you're half the man I think you are, I expect to be best man at your wedding."

"Hickok," Sundance said.

Hickok stopped. "What?"

"You tricked me, didn't you? You never intended to draw. You just wanted me so rattled you could have your say without me interrupting. Am I right?" Sundance queried.

Hickok chuckled. "I'll never tell."

Sundance grinned. "I'm beginning to understand the reason for your reputation. It's well deserved. You're one shrewd Warrior."

Hickok raised his right forefinger over his lips. "Shhh! Don't let Geronimo hear you saying that! He thinks I'm an idiot, and I'd like to keep it that way."

Sundance laughed. "I'll never tell."

"And give some thought to Bertha, will you?" Hickok mentioned as he began to stroll off.

"I will," Sundance promised.

"One more thing," Hickok said, looking over his right shoulder.

"What?" Sundance responded.

"You can put those Grizzlies away, unless you want me to find you a sparrow to shoot."

Three months later Sundance and Bertha were married in an elaborate Family ceremony. Hickok served as best man.

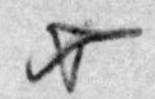